BAKEMONOGATARI

MONSTER TALE

PART 03

NISIOISIN

VERTICAL.

BAKEMONOGATARI
Monster Tale

Part 03

NISIOISIN

Art by VOFAN

Translated by Ko Ransom

VERTICAL.

CHAPTER FIVE   TSUBASA CAT

BAKEMONOGATARI, PART 03

First published in Japan in 2006
by Kodansha Ltd., Tokyo.
Publication rights for this English
edition arranged through
Kodansha Ltd., Tokyo.

Published by Vertical, Inc., New York,
2017

ISBN 978-1-942993-90-2

Manufactured in the United States
of America

First Edition

Vertical, Inc.
451 Park Avenue South, 7th Floor
New York, NY 10016

www.vertical-inc.com

CHAPTER FIVE
TSUBASA CAT

TSUBASA HANEKAWA

001

Tsubasa Hanekawa is a very important person to me. No one, no thing could ever hope to replace her. I owe her a lot—no, I nearly owe her everything. I doubt I can ever repay this debt of gratitude, no matter what I do for her. When she reached her hand out to me as every part of my body and soul experienced what felt like the deepest and darkest of depths during spring break, it was as if I saw, and I am not exaggerating in the slightest, the hand of a goddess offering me salvation. Even now, when I recall what happened about two months ago, I feel something hot welling up in my chest. Talk about one person saving another might sound contrived on second thought, but I still believe that Tsubasa Hanekawa saved me that spring break. If there's any belief or feeling I have that I would call steadfast, this is it. Which is why—which is why once my personal hell of a spring break came to an end and I started my third year of high school and was placed in the same class as her, I won't lie, I was so happy I was almost grinning. Not to bring up a line Senjogahara used on me once, but I wondered if that was how it felt to be placed in the same class as your unrequited crush. Even when she forced me to take on the position of class vice president due to a little misunderstanding after she was voted class president, I accepted it without much protest, only because Hanekawa was that important a person to me.

Tsubasa Hanekawa.

The girl whose first name means "wing," and whose last name starts with another character for the same, a pair of mismatched appendages.

Then again, it wasn't as if I had never heard the name Tsubasa Hanekawa until my second-year spring break—I confess that I snuck over to get a peek at her class when I was a first-year, hoping to catch a glimpse of the most gifted young lady in the history of Naoetsu Private High School. Even at that time her appearance, glasses with her hair neatly braided, bangs in front, pegged her as a model student. I could tell at once that she took school seriously. People who look smart aren't entirely rare, but that was the first time I ever saw someone who had to be smart. You hesitated to say a casual word to her, that's how solemn and dignified a freshman she was. She wasn't hard to approach as much as a thing apart that you weren't permitted to stare at even from a distance. I'd pushed myself too hard to get into Naoetsu High, so I was already starting to understand my position at the school, but you know, maybe it was the moment when I saw Tsubasa Hanekawa that it really sank in. Not only had she never ceded the title of top of her class, she apparently hadn't been left in the dust when it came to anything related to grades since her time in elementary school. It was hard to believe that she and I belonged to the same species.

That isn't to say Tsubasa Hanekawa is stuck-up, she's nothing of the kind. I wouldn't want you to get that impression because I've never met a more decent human being, in fact. I'm afraid I actually misunderstood her until last spring break, but when I spoke to her up close and in person, she seemed to address everyone on almost excessively even ground, to the point that I felt she needed to be more self-aware of her skills and talent. The so-called model students at Naoetsu Private High School tend to consider smarts as something you use to differentiate yourself from others, but not Tsubasa Hanekawa. That sense of being a thing apart that I got when I first saw her was totally not her own view. It turns out she is fair, and open. A class president among class presidents, a class president elected by the gods themselves—the school seems to like her, plus she is popular in class. She has a serious personality, but more than that, she is caring. It can get out of hand and yield misbegotten assumptions like the one that made her appoint me vice president, but that's about the only fault I can find with her. I'll admit that working with her as class president and vice president has its fair share of annoyances, but more often I'm impressed by her character.

I realize it may not be the best way to put this, but it's incredible considering her family situation, which I learned during Golden Week—the nine days from April 29th to Sunday, May 7th, which is where the vacation fell this year. If my spring break was like hell, those nine days were like a nightmare, the memories of which Tsubasa Hanekawa herself has already forgotten. To the extent that dreams are something that you usually don't remember, "nightmare" seems quite appropriate.

For nine days.

She was bewitched by a cat.

Just like I was attacked by a demon, she was bewitched by a cat. There's a fitting reason for every aberration—and in this case, the strained and warped family life that she was bearing was it. Yes, speaking of misunderstandings, it was a huge misunderstanding. Until then, maybe I saw the world in black and white and believed that good people are happy people and that bad people are unhappy people. That there might be people whose unhappiness gives them no choice but to be decent—I hadn't been able to wrap my head around so simple a notion.

And yet.

Tsubasa Hanekawa reached her hand out to me.

That spring break, too, she couldn't have been in a place to be helping me—yet she pulled me out of the deepest depths.

I won't forget that.

No matter what may happen.

0 0 2

"Oh…Big Brother Koyomi. I was waiting for you."

"………"

I'd been waited for.

After classes were over on Tuesday, June thirteenth, which promised to become a memorable day for me, I used every minute available after school to prepare for the last culture festival of my high school career that weekend, and the time was a little past six-thirty p.m., the place the front gates of Naoetsu Private High School. There, looking bored as she waited for me, was Nadeko Sengoku, one of my younger sister's old friends, with whom I'd spent several aberration-related hours until the morning of that day, along with my junior Suruga Kanbaru.

The girl was wearing—a school uniform.

A middle school uniform that took me back.

Her uniform was a dress, rare for these parts.

She had a belt clasped around her waist—to which she'd attached a small pouch. And yes, given the circumstances, it only made sense, but I realized it was my first time ever seeing her in uniform. The dress looked good on Sengoku, with her generally childish appearance.

She wasn't wearing a hat.

Her eyes, though, were still hidden by her long bangs. It seemed to be her default hairstyle… Whether it was pulling her hat down or letting her bangs overhang her face, she seemed thoroughly shy about

13

making eye contact or even letting others see hers. Her shyness approached historic levels.

"H-Hey there."

My greeting rang somewhat hollow, Sengoku's sudden appearance having surprised me more than you'd expect. She was standing in the gate's shadows, and her timing had been like a "Boo!" from someone lurking in a corner, though I was sure that wasn't her intention.

"What're you doing over here?" I asked.

"Oh, uh…Big Brother Koyomi."

Sengoku seemed to be looking away from me as she spoke.

With her hair covering her eyes, I couldn't even tell if she was.

Did she, at least, see me from in there?

Hmm… I have to admit, being called "Big Brother Koyomi" right outside of my own school was somewhat embarrassing… But if I told her to stop calling me that, I ran the risk of hurting Sengoku, who was as delicate as a newborn fawn…

While my reaction to seeing her was surprise, seeing me clearly put her at ease. Naturally, it took a decent amount of resolve for a second-year middle school student just to visit a high school, but she'd been feeling way more frightened than necessary. I couldn't deal her a final blow… Luckily, the time of day was on our side. I'd stayed at school late, even among the students preparing for the culture festival, so the chance of any I knew passing by was close to nil. If someone did, my nickname would most definitely become "Big Brother Koyomi," but the risk had to be slim.

"U-Um," Sengoku said before falling silent.

I knew that she wasn't talkative and that I had to bear the silence. If I couldn't stand it and tried to fill the void, she'd just clam up even more. Still, and this is only a figure of speech, it was as if I was dealing with a timid little creature like a rabbit or a hamster…

Hmm.

It made me want to spoil her.

"I wanted to…thank you again," she said at last. "You…really helped me."

"Ah, I see… You were waiting all this time not knowing when I'd leave, just to tell me that? How long have you been here? If you came right after middle school—"

"Oh, no. I took today off. From school."

"Huh?"

Right, of course.

Being in uniform didn't mean that she'd been to school.

"Okay, so you didn't go there afterwards."

"No...I was sleepy."

"......"

That line on its own, well, it made her sound like the carefree princess of some tropical island... While she'd technically gotten some shut-eye at the abandoned cram school the night before, in that awful environment, with only a plastic bottle as a pillow and other people right beside her, no wonder the utterly delicate Sengoku couldn't sleep well. Even I couldn't and went back to bed after getting home... Kanbaru was the weird one to sleep soundly in that environment. So then, afterwards, Sengoku had gone home and fallen asleep just like me— but unable to get back up, unlike me—had come to these school gates around the time I would be leaving. It was a weekday, and the uniform must have been her attempt to ward off any truancy officers.

"Yikes, today was the worst timing," I said to her. "Didn't I tell you? This high school is having a culture festival over the weekend, and we're right in the middle of getting ready for it. Which is why I ended up leaving so late, my bad. Um, did I actually make you wait for more than two hours?"

"N-No." Sengoku shook her head.

Huh? Classes normally ended at half past three, so I'd come up with that number assuming that she arrived at around four... Could she have gone off somewhere in between because I was taking so long?

"I started waiting at around two, so it's been more than four hours..."

"What are you, stupid?!"

I ended up shouting at her with everything I had.

Waiting in front of the gates for over four hours... If anything, the uniform made her seem all the more suspicious in that case. It's not like

15

any high school's classes finished at two. What were the security guards the place spent a fortune on doing all that time? Feeling soothed by a cute middle schooler?

"I-I'm sorry for being stupid."

I'd been apologized to.

I'd never been apologized to before for such a reason…

"Still…I wanted to thank you… I just wanted to so much…so much that I couldn't sit still…"

"What an upright girl you are…"

The word I really wanted to use was uptight.

To thank me, huh?

"In that case," I said, "you should be thanking Kanbaru. She must have passed by here already, right? Did you not meet her? You and I *are* old acquaintances, while she did everything she could for you when you two barely had anything to do with each other. There aren't a whole lot of people out there like her."

In more ways than one.

I won't go into detail, but it was the absolute truth that Kanbaru had worked selflessly to solve Sengoku's case.

"Yes…I thought so, too," Sengoku said timidly. "You and Miss Kanbaru saved me at the cost of your lives—"

"Hold on, hold on! We didn't exactly sacrifice our lives to save you! Look, I'm alive right now!"

"Oh…that's true."

"Don't just say stuff guided by your feelings…out of the blue like that."

"Yes… So I wanted to thank Miss Kanbaru again, too, but…"

"Huh? Oh, has Kanbaru not come by yet? I thought my class was the last to leave…but I guess it's second-years who can put the most into culture festivals. First-years don't know how things work, while third-years are busy preparing for entrance exams. She does seem like the type to find herself at the center of her class whether she likes it or not…"

"N-No. Miss Kanbaru came by here just half an hour ago or so."

"Oh, she did? You didn't call out to her because she was with her friends or something? She must have many."

16

"No...she was alone, but..." Sengoku made a difficult face. "Before I could say anything, she ran past me so fast I almost couldn't see her..."

"......"

Kanbaru must have been in a rush...

I assumed it was to do something immeasurably sublime, like finish reading the mountain of boys' love novels she'd bought the day before, but Sengoku, who hesitated even to catch the attention of people she knew well, wasn't going to stand in the way of a running Suruga Kanbaru.

"I thought she might run me over..."

"Yeah, I understand... I really do. I wouldn't dare call out to Kanbaru while she's speeding, either."

"Yes... It was as if she was using *takkyudo*."

"Why would you compare something she did to a special attack used by Prince Yamato, one of the main characters in *Bikkuriman*, of all things?! Not only are you making the situation harder to understand, you're forcing my retort to essentially be straight commentary!"

"Yes... I didn't think you'd get it."

She seemed honestly surprised.

Man, it appeared as though she'd underestimated my abilities as the designated quipper... Okay, wrong thing to be boasting about.

"Still, middle school girls these days know about *Bikkuriman*? Maybe the characters' names thanks to the new set of chocolates they've been selling, but the names of special attacks?"

"I watched it on DVD."

"Ah, I see... We live in such a world of convenience. But either way, that's a difficult reference to get. You could have at least compared it to a flash step."

"Flash step... Um, is that when...flashing images begin to look like motion?"

"That's called persistence of vision!"

"Oh, is it? But they're similar."

"Not one bit! Don't lump together one of the most closely guarded secrets in all of martial arts and a basic optical illusion!"

When I yelled at Sengoku, she turned her back to me, and her shoulders began to quake. I fretted that my harsh comeback had made her cry, until I realized that she was desperately stifling a laugh. She was gasping for breath.

Right, she was quick to laugh.

Even when she was part of the exchange, it seemed.

"Big Brother Koyomi…you're as funny as ever…"

So she said.

…I couldn't remember well, but had that been my role as far back as elementary school?

The thought was kind of depressing…

Either way, Sengoku had it in her to be a fun conversation partner, after all. Maybe I wasn't going all out with my comebacks, but I was quipping just fine. In fact, she'd been at the peak of her aberration troubles the day before…maybe she simply hadn't had the necessary peace of mind. I was starting to want to test this introverted girl's ability to draw out my skills.

She confided, "I was worried her shoes might not last if she ran at that kind of speed…but Miss Kanbaru did look very cool when she was running."

"You'd better not fall for her. I don't mean to take back what I said, but she's a handful in her own way. I will admit, she's as cool as they ever come nowadays… Fine, I'll set up a chance for you to thank her properly, so you can—"

"Y-Yes. But…I also had another reason to see Miss Kanbaru."

"You did?"

"Yes."

"Hmm…"

I couldn't think of any business Sengoku might have with Kanbaru other than thanking her, but then again, they'd spent no small amount of time together. Maybe they had made some kind of promise.

"If you want," I offered, "I could handle it for you. I need to go thank Kanbaru, myself."

Sengoku's case—the case of Sengoku's snake.

Had Kanbaru not gotten involved—it was dubious whether I'd be standing there talking with Sengoku. It had to be irritating to be on the receiving end of the same repeated apologies and thanks, but one last show of gratitude once we'd both settled back down didn't seem out of the question.

"But..." said Sengoku, "I'd be bothering you."

"Don't stand on ceremony. I wouldn't even think of it as a chore, so leave it to me."

"Oh...then maybe I'll ask you, Big Brother."

Sengoku took two small, folded pieces of clothing out from the bag she carried.

Volleyball shorts and a school swimsuit.

"........."

Forget not having thought of them, I'd erased every trace of that business from my memory...

"I washed them, and wanted to give them back to Miss Kanbaru when I saw her...but if you can return them for me, please do. The sooner the better, after all."

"Yeah..."

What a high bar!

Now this was a trial.

A guy receiving volleyball shorts and a school swimsuit from a middle school girl right outside his high school... If anyone I knew saw me, my nickname would somersault past "Big Brother Koyomi" and be, without question, "Pervert"!

But given our conversation, I couldn't say no!

If this was a trap someone had set for me, how clever it was! O heavenly lord, the tribulations you force upon me!

"O-Okay...I'll hold onto these."

Sure that I'd never see another occasion to receive the like, I took the two articles of clothing from Sengoku. As she handed them to me, for a brief moment she seemed somehow reluctant (perhaps she felt that she ought to return them herself, after all), but in the end she let go.

Hmmm.

This was a somewhat strange turn of events, though.

Today—was supposed to become memorable for me.

As our conversation ended, Sengoku began to blush, her eyes to the ground. Freed from the snake aberration, the gloom that enveloped her had thinned, but her naturally quiet nature seemed unchanged.

On a vague impulse.

I reached out toward Sengoku's bangs.

"...Wha?"

I missed.

My hand touched nothing but air. Sengoku had pulled her downcast head to the side to elude me. I went after her bangs again, on another vague impulse, but this time she took a step back to shun my pursuit.

"...Wh-What's wrong?" I asked.

"I dunno, just..."

Did she have to act so bothered?

These were quick movements that you'd never expect from the usually mild-mannered Sengoku. They say bangs can diminish your vision, but it didn't seem to be an issue for her at all.

"...Hmm."

I thought I'd try something.

I slipped my other hand downward to grab the hem of her one-piece uniform. The way she'd moved to keep me from touching her bangs reminded me of how a grade school girl might evade attempts to flip her skirt, so I was conducting a little experiment.

Yet Sengoku didn't react to that hand. All she did was tilt her head to the side, as if she found it strange.

A thought came to me that I'd also had the day before.

This girl was far too pure for a middle schooler...

She was defending herself in all the wrong places.

I let go of her uniform right away.

"Facing you," I said, "feels like a test of my mettle as a man..."

"...Because I don't talk very much?"

"No, it's not that..."

Because she doesn't talk much, huh...

Oh...speaking of which.

"That's right, Sengoku—there was something I wanted to ask you. May I?"

"Hm? What is it?"

"Nothing big… It's about Shinobu."

"Shinobu?"

"You know, that cute little blond girl at the ruined cram school. Maybe I never told you her name. Whatever. Anyway, did she say anything to you when I wasn't around?"

"………?"

Sengoku made a puzzled face like she didn't understand the point of my question before going ahead and replying in the negative.

"Uh-uh."

Okay.

Well, I'd expected as much… I thought there might be some kind of shared ground between two silent girls, but upon further consideration, there was none between Shinobu, who used to be loquacious, and Sengoku, who'd always been taciturn…

Shinobu Oshino.

Blond hair and a helmet with a pair of goggles on top.

The beautiful girl who, along with Mèmè Oshino, my savior, currently called that abandoned cram school home—though their life there was too hollow to describe it as a home.

"That girl…is a vampire, right?" asked Sengoku.

It wasn't something I could hide if I were to heal the wounds I'd suffered from exorcising her snake, so I'd already told her last night before going to bed with plastic bottles as our pillows. Since she'd been told about Kanbaru's left arm to an extent as well, I didn't have to tread lightly on the topic of aberrations around Sengoku.

Except when it came to Hachikuji.

And Hanekawa—but that aside.

"Ah… Well, now," I answered, "she's more like a mockery of a vampire than an actual vampire."

Just as I was more a mockery of a human than an actual human.

That—was who she was.

"So it's because of her—that you…"

"It wasn't anything she did," I denied. "I did it to myself. And—it'd be a mistake to hold aberrations accountable for anything. All they do is *exist as they are*."

There's a reason for every aberration.

It's as simple as that.

"Yes, you're…right," Sengoku agreed with a solemn nod.

She seemed to be thinking about my words in relation to her own case. According to Oshino, hers had quite a different significance from the other instances I'd experienced until then, so it wouldn't do to generalize…

"But unlike me and Kanbaru," I said, "you've been completely freed from your aberration. You shouldn't worry yourself too much about it. All you need to do is go back to living a normal life."

Because you—can go back.

She had to go back.

"Yes… That's true, but now, I know that these things happen…that these things exist…and I doubt I can pretend that I don't."

"……"

Well, yes—I doubted anyone could.

It wasn't as if Sengoku was uniquely timid. All in all, not many people are able to fight on a field where the rules of common sense don't apply. Maybe in that regard, taking a step toward that world and staying there, like Kanbaru and me, was easier on you.

"For the time being," I advised, "stay the hell away from ridiculous curses—that's all I can say."

"Yes…"

"I feel like Oshino said that people who become involved with aberrations are more likely to draw their attention again, but still, it has to do with your mindset. It sounds like things can balance out if you choose to avoid them. Well, just talk to me if anything happens. Did I give you my cell phone number?"

"Oh… No, not yet."

I don't have a cell phone, anyway, she said.

Right, maybe she'd told me that before.

"But," I insisted, "you could still call me on mine. Here, take this down."

"Okay…"

Sengoku looked bashful.

She also seemed somehow happy. Could it be that getting someone's cell phone number felt pretty grownup to her? She was in her second year of junior high, when you start wanting to act more mature. Of course, since I don't have many friends and actually feel a little nervous when I exchange numbers even now, it's not like I had any right to be poking fun at Sengoku.

She wrote my number on a fancy notepad that she carefully placed back in her waist bag. Wearing such a bag definitely clashed with her uniform, but she'd had it on even when I met her in the mountains, so it had to be a favorite item of hers.

"Then—let me give you my home number in return," she said.

"Much appreciated."

"If you need help, please call me, okay?"

"Uhh… Do you see that ever happening?"

"Big Brother Koyomi."

"Yeah, yeah, whatever. I will."

"You only need to say 'yes' once."

"Do I now? But actually, if you're ever in serious trouble, it'd be quicker if you went straight to Oshino… Though I guess a middle school girl visiting a shabby old dude unaccompanied is a little much."

That awful man making an exception for Sengoku and acting oddly generous was still bugging me. It was probably nothing, but I wouldn't want her going to that abandoned building alone, just in case.

Pedo suspect Mèmè Oshino…

"I-I don't think…" stuttered Sengoku, "it'd be a problem."

"Yeah, maybe not. But he just reminded me. We can't go to him for every little thing that happens—like in that anime, always counting on Doraemon and his secret gadgets will make you as helpless as Nobita."

"Y…es." Sengoku nodded. "That amulet Mister Oshino gave us really was like a Doraemon device… Yup, like the Genius Helmet and Technology Gloves."

"Why go out of your way to choose obscure ones that only ever appeared in the theatrical feature for your comparison?! Why not the Bamboo-Copter or the Anywhere Door?!"

"Wow, your comebacks are always so timely and precise…"

Sengoku seemed impressed.

The light of respect gleamed in her eyes.

What a thing to be respected for…

"By the way," she continued.

"What?"

"People say that in the movie versions of *Doraemon*, Giant suddenly becomes a weirdly grownup and good-natured character, but shouldn't they be saying that about Nobita more than anyone?"

"Where did that even come from?!"

"Huh? I don't feel like I spoke out of context."

"It might be connected, but it's *only* connected! It's a total tangent! Why would you go into greater depth about the *Doraemon* movies?!"

Though she was right, Giant barely grows at all in the films compared to the progress Nobita makes!

"I think," she said, "Suneo is the one character who never experiences any growth, no matter what."

"True, given his positioning as the local bully's sidekick, it'd be hard for him to change, even in a negative direction… Wait, why are we going on about this?!"

At that, Sengoku fell silent.

She wasn't trying to stifle a laugh this time. She really seemed down. Oh no, maybe I'd gone a little too far… Maybe she'd been trying her best, her quiet-person best to keep the conversation going, and yet, childishly enough, I'd yelled at her even if it was to play the straight man.

"I'm sorry," Sengoku eventually said.

Agh. I felt awful.

"No, it's not anything you need to apologize for…"

"I wanted to see how far you'd go making retorts, and I got carried away…"

"Well, if that's the case, you ought to be saying a lot more sorries!"

She was the one testing me?!

My quipping was unlimited, but my patience was.

Look at this introverted girl, having her fun.

"When I said 'by the way,' I actually wasn't planning on talking

24

about *Doraemon*."

"Oh… Aren't you the little improviser. Okay, start again from there."

"Okay. By the way."

"What?"

"Well, it's about Shinobu."

Sengoku didn't seem to know that repetition was key to playing the fool in a comedy duo, so she actually went back to the meat of our conversation instead of continuing to talk about *Doraemon*.

Hmm. I felt somehow unsatisfied.

If it were Hachikuji, she might have gone beyond repetition and even come up with something snappy to turn the tables.

Maybe we'd touched the limits of Sengoku's abilities.

"What about her? You two didn't talk."

"No, but…" Sengoku said, "that girl was glaring at me the whole time."

"…? Oh, don't worry about that. She's always looking at people that way. She glares like crazy. At me, and at Oshino, and at Kanbaru. It's not just you, Sengoku."

Getting stared at by a vampire, even a child vampire, might have been tough on the timid Sengoku. Then again, even I find that gaze dreadful, filled as it is with the kind of spite you'd expect from the classic ghost of Oiwa… So much more Nadeko Sengoku.

But she said, "No. I know that she glares at everyone… But she doesn't look at me and Miss Kanbaru the same way she looks at you and Mister Oshino—I thought."

"…Hm?" What the heck? I didn't get it. "You're saying she looks at men and women in different ways?"

"Yes… That's it."

"Huh."

"I'm…sensitive to the way people look at me, so I can tell… It felt like for some reason, she hates Miss Kanbaru and me."

"She hates you? That's funny."

Maybe not funny, but strange.

"Impossible" would be another way to put it.

Despite her current cute-kid appearance, on the inside she was an aberration, period, and at bottom she was a vampire, period—she basically wasn't interested in humans. Whether it was Sengoku or Kanbaru, or me or Oshino, she'd see everyone the same way. I wasn't sure if she actually differentiated between men and women.

Likes and dislikes, on top of that?

…Well.

I was an exception—maybe.

"But Sengoku, if you say so, I believe you… Why would that be, though? Maybe I'll try asking Oshino next time I see him."

"Mister Oshino? You're not going to ask Shinobu directly?"

"She used to talk a lot, you know," I said with a bitter smile. It was the only expression I had for the situation, really. "But now she's closed her heart off and locked it tight. I haven't heard her voice in over two months now. She's kept mum the whole time."

For over two months—ever since spring break.

Not a word had come from her mouth.

I hadn't checked, because what would be the point, but I assumed it was the same for Oshino.

It couldn't be helped.

There was no helping it.

"I see…"

"I find it impressive," I said. "She has to have a lot to say, but she's keeping it all in. Especially when it comes to me, there's probably no end to what she'd like to tell me, and yet—"

Like her resentment.

Like her hatred.

She had to be bursting with it—but never put it into words.

Or maybe there were no words for how she felt, but she never confronted me with those unspeakable feelings, either.

"…Isn't it the other way around?" asked Sengoku, puzzled. "Aren't you actually the victim—"

"I'm the guilty one," I interrupted. "I really am when it comes to Shinobu—I was a bigger perpetrator than you were a victim, Sengoku. I'd prefer not to go into details, if we could—but please, at the very least, don't blame Shinobu for it."

"Oh, okay…"

Sengoku nodded, but looked somewhat dissatisfied. I couldn't fault her for not understanding how things stood between Shinobu and me, though. Even I don't, not all that well.

There is one thing I do get.

I have to devote my whole life to Shinobu—because that's the only way I, the guilty one, can atone for what I did.

Still—even though it can't be helped.

Still, I do think.

I can't help but think.

Will I never hear that vampire's beautiful voice—ever again?

"Well." To shatter the oppressive mood that was starting to come over us, I spoke in an upbeat tone. "It might be best if you never met Oshino or Shinobu again. It might be hard going back to life as usual when you know about these aberrations, but knowing also means you can work to avoid them."

"Uh, yes… But I still need to thank Mister Oshino, too…"

"Hmm. I have a feeling he doesn't really like that kind of thing… But you're right. Never seeing him again might be for the best, but it does seem like a sad choice. Some tie must have brought you together."

Not that I knew how to feel about ties wrought by an aberration.

…Then again.

Maybe I shouldn't say that.

Hanekawa and I, Senjogahara and I, Hachikuji and I, Kanbaru and I—those were all ties brought about by aberrations. I knew how I felt about them.

The same went for my reunion with Sengoku.

"Say," I added, "we were in a rush yesterday, and the situation being what it was, you were forced to hide, but you should see my little sister again sometime. I asked and she still remembers you."

"O-Oh, really? Rara does?"

"Yep. So come to our house to play again when you have a chance."

"Is that okay? I can go to your room and play, Big Brother Koyomi?"

"Yeah."

Wait, it'd be an issue if she came to my room…

Our house, please, not my room.

"Wh-When? When can I?"

"Hmm. Well, I guess after the culture festival is over—"

Just then.

As I was mentally flipping through my upcoming schedule—

"Oh, Araragi, it's you," a voice came from behind me. "What are you doing out here?"

I turned to find Hanekawa.

Tsubasa Hanekawa.

My class's class president—the model student who'd been hard at work preparing for the culture festival with me until just a while ago. It'd been my turn today to return the classroom key to the teacher's lounge, and she should have gone home before me, so why was she walking up to me from behind?

Jogging up to me and coming around to my front, Hanekawa discovered Sengoku. Prior to exiting through the school gates, Hanekawa hadn't seen the girl hiding behind my body.

"Oh… Um?"

"Ah. Hanekawa, this is the girl I told you about yesterday—" I began.

"E, e-e-e-e-excuse me!"

Pardoning herself in an utterly cracked voice, Sengoku turned tail and—while I'd never say it put Kanbaru to shame, the burst of speed did remind me of her—dashed away from the front gates of Naoetsu Private High School.

It was only a few seconds before she vanished from sight.

If anyone ever darted off like a hare, she had.

……

She took her people-phobia a little too far…

Are high schoolers really so frightening, Sengoku?

If this is how she was going to act around Hanekawa, how was I ever going to introduce her to Senjogahara? I'd considered inviting Sengoku to the culture festival depending on how things played out, but it didn't look like she'd be able to set foot on the premises of a high school…

"Araragi," Hanekawa said after a moment. "You know, I think that kind of hurt…"

"Yeah…"

No matter how gentle and tolerant Hanekawa was, she'd have to object to someone running off after nothing more than seeing her face—I bore little if any responsibility for the situation, but I still found myself feeling bad about it.

"Didn't you go home before me?" I asked.

"I got tied up talking to Hoshina in the hall."

"I see."

Hoshina, our homeroom teacher.

Hanekawa was widely loved, after all.

"Er," I began, "sorry I didn't introduce you sooner, but…" By now it was too late. The person was already gone. "That girl just now is my little sister's friend that I told you about yesterday. Her name is Nadeko Sengoku, and she's in her second year of junior high school."

"Huh… Oh, right. I wanted to ask you, Araragi—about, um, that snake. Whatever happened with the aberration?"

So it was weighing on her after all.

I did leave a lot of things up in the air when I talked to her about it yesterday.

"Well," I replied, "it got solved—though we ended up having to rely on Oshino yet again."

"Hm. I don't really understand, but okay, that was a quick resolution. So all it took was yesterday to close the case."

"I wouldn't say it's open and shut…but sure, something like that. She was waiting here all this time because she wanted to thank me and Kanbaru. What a sorry girl."

"That isn't something you ought to say about a person who went out of their way to thank you, Araragi."

"Hey, that was just a manner of speaking—" I started to make an excuse for myself.

But then I stopped.

"Well, you're right. I shouldn't have been sarcastic."

"Very good," Hanekawa said, looking satisfied.

It was almost as if I'd been domesticated by her.

"She was an awfully cute girl, though. Sengoku, you said? Nadeko Sengoku. I want to say that uniform is from the middle school you graduated from."

"You know everything, don't you?"

"Not everything. I just know what I know."

"Uh huh."

Sure.

I guessed I could see her knowing that.

"I don't know, though, Sengoku seemed incredibly shy…"

"Yeah… She's so shy that she'd bring her own bag to the grocery store just because she's too scared to answer a clerk when she gets asked 'paper or plastic.'"

If you're curious, that was entirely my own preconception of her.

I wasn't saying it to put her down for no reason. I needed us to be able to laugh off her sudden escape, or else I'd feel bad for Hanekawa.

"Ahaha. Araragi, whether it's Senjogahara or Kanbaru or Mayoi, you've been getting along with a whole bunch of cute girls lately."

"Don't put it that way, you're making it sound like there are more than just those three."

"There aren't?"

"Nope," I asserted, but it was a lie.

There was at least one more.

Tsubasa Hanekawa.

There's you.

"Hm? What?" she asked.

"Nothing…"

I mean, if I called Hanekawa a cute girl to her face, she'd probably treat it as a simple act of sexual harassment… There was no need for me to incriminate myself.

"By the way, Araragi."

"Yeah?"

"Didn't you say you had something to do today? I thought that's why you were in such a rush to go return the classroom key… Don't tell me that important business of yours was a chat with a cute middle school girl."

"No."

"My impression of you as a ladies' man gets stronger every day, Araragi."

"No, it's not that…" This was actually something that caused me distress. Hanekawa, at least, might get it. "I was being vague about it earlier, but I'll explain because I don't want you to misunderstand. The 'something important' I need to do involves Senjogahara. I didn't want to tell you because it was embarrassing, that's all."

"Senjogahara, huh?"

Hmm, Hanekawa said with a doubtful expression.

As president, Hanekawa had to be frowning on a classmate who, even with the culture festival right around the corner, skipped out on any and all preparations with nothing more than an "I'm going to the hospital." That was, of course, a big lie coming from Senjogahara, who was nothing close to ill, regardless of what may have been the case before. Then again, this was Hanekawa—who just maybe saw through it. Actually, I felt like Senjogahara was overplaying that perceived trait of hers and it was wearing thin…

"Want to hear an interesting rumor?" Hanekawa asked.

"What is it? Doesn't sound interesting, but I'll listen."

"Senjogahara has been acting weird ever since you became friends with her."

"Urk."

"You're a bad influence on Senjogahara."

"Urrk."

"That kind of thing."

"Urrrk."

What the hell.

Rumors?

"Hoshina just asked me, 'Do you know anything, Hanekawa?'"

"Ungh…"

It was an irresponsible rumor—of course it was.

But while it was unpleasant, I couldn't find it in myself to get upset… I felt like it was partially true, or at least I could understand why

31

people might say that.

"I might've also been told that someone did or didn't witness you walking arm-in-arm with Kanbaru, the second-year, on Sunday."

"Nkk."

That one was true.

Still, what a small town I lived in…

One full of snitches, too.

Hanekawa continued, "I don't know exactly what caused you to become so friendly with Senjogahara—but I do think that more and more people are going to say that kind of thing about you from now on."

"Yeah—they probably will."

"So it's going to be difficult. You're going to have to prove that none of it is true."

"……"

"You can't have people saying unflattering things about Senjogahara—like she's been no good after she started seeing a guy. I don't think it's fine for you to be talking to a cute middle school girl in front of the school gates."

"…You're right."

I had nothing to say for myself.

Senjogahara being cast in a poor light because of me was unacceptable. That might sound conceited, but I had to feel at least that much responsible for her.

"Say, Hanekawa. Aren't there any about you?"

"Hm?"

"Those kinds of rumors. Like acting weird ever since you became friends with me."

"Who knows. Even if there were, no one's going to tell me to my face. Though I do doubt it. I don't ever change, after all."

"………"

She was right.

If any rumors did exist, they'd be the opposite—Araragi's behavior improving ever since he became friends with Hanekawa, or something along those lines.

And that one—was also true.

It was hard to express just how much she saved me.

"Anyway, I did deny it," she informed me. "I said I didn't think any of that was true."

"Oh. Thanks."

"There's no need to thank me. I spoke my mind, that's all."

"Ah. But do you really feel that way?"

"Huh?"

"That—none of it is true."

"Oh. Yeah, of course. I've never lied before in my life."

"You might be the only person I know who dares to say that who isn't a liar."

"Really? There must be plenty. Yes, that's right—if anything, I think Senjogahara is headed in a good direction."

Though I don't think it's good for her to be skipping out on work—Hanekawa said. So it was obvious to her that Senjogahara was lying. In fact, how would you ever hope to hide something from a class president who knows everything?

"I'm not sure whether it was getting over her illness or thanks to you—but you do need to stand by her to support her as she changes."

"…That doesn't sound like anything a high schooler would say, you know that?"

"Really? It's just normal."

"Okay."

One of Tsubasa Hanekawa's unique traits was her conviction that she was "normal"…but if she was normal, what rank in the world did I occupy?

A thought came to me.

For a while now, and that included the present moment, this class president here had a lot of opinions regarding the subtleties of romance and relations between the sexes, but did she have someone like that of her own at all?

She was kind to everyone—but.

Did she have a special someone?

I never even got a hint of that being the case, but maybe serious girls like her did have a proper partner. Or didn't. Hmm, I hadn't thought about it...

"Hey, Hanekawa—"

"Yes?" she asked in reply, puzzled.

Agh...

I couldn't do it. I couldn't ask...

If I may borrow a page from Sengoku and make a *Bikkuriman* reference, merely mouthing such a question felt impure when Tsubasa Hanekawa was bathing me in the powerful white light of seriousness that she gave off naturally as if she were Arrow Angel.

"What is it, Araragi?" she asked again with an innocuous look.

Gah... I didn't know why, but it was like I'd been cornered. Was this how the culprit felt right before he got pushed into confessing by a famed detective? Damn, an "actually, never mind" wasn't going to work on her now that I started to ask, not with the way she is. I needed to pose a question. Ack, I was regretting this no less than the time I tried using two different-colored bath bombs.

"Uh, well, those secret gadgets that Doraemon uses—"

Having run out of options, I turned to *Doraemon* talk as a last resort but was only halfway through when Hanekawa interrupted me with a murmur.

"Ouch."

Ouch... Was she talking about me? Was she cringing because I, a high school senior, was bringing up *Doraemon* (and as a desperate measure, at that)? Even though it was fine for middle schoolers?

I was consumed by paranoid thoughts for a moment, but no, Hanekawa had her fingertips to her head. In other words—she probably had a headache. And while much of the previous day had blurred together, what with how messy it had been, she did say something like that then, too...

"Hey—are you okay?"

"Yes... Yes, I am," Hanekawa assured me.

The smile she pointed in my direction was indeed unclouded—but that would mean her earlier utterance was false.

I've never lied before in my life?

Just look, though—that was a lie.

"We could go to the nurse's room—no, Harukami must have left by now, too. In that case, we could go to a hospital—"

"I said I'm okay. You're overreacting, Araragi. All I have to do is go home and study a bit for it to go away."

"You seriously believe that studying cures headaches…"

She was, quite simply, bizarre about these things.

She thought in different ways from the rest of us.

"You said it's been happening a lot lately, right? What if it's something terrible?"

"You're worrying too much. You can be pretty lily-livered sometimes, you know? Forget about that, Araragi. Do you understand what I told you? And understanding me isn't enough. You need to put it into practice, too."

"Yeah, I get it."

Forget about that.

Putting others ahead of yourself.

On that point, too—I thought she was a weirdo.

But.

"Sorry for making you fuss over me so much," I said.

"It's not like I mind. But anyway, if you understand what I'm trying to tell you, Araragi…" Hanekawa let out what sounded like a forced cough before continuing, "Why not start by putting away those volleyball shorts and school swimsuit you're cradling like some kind of treasure?"

003

June thirteenth, a memorable day for me.

It was supposed to become one.

And it had absolutely nothing to do with volleyball shorts, school swimsuits, or the like. It all started with a remark by Hitagi Senjogahara, my girlfriend as of Mother's Day last month, May fourteenth.

"I'll go on a date."

It happened that afternoon during our lunch break.

The words came from nowhere as we sat on a courtyard bench side by side and ate our lunches in what must have looked like a couple-like scene. I was so astonished that I dropped the rolled omelet that I was picking up with my chopsticks.

Excuse me?

What did this woman just say?

I glanced at Senjogahara.

She wore her summer uniform.

A fad was quietly beginning to take off among the girls at my school where they took the already short sleeves of their uniforms, folded them back even further, and pinned them there to make it look like they were wearing sleeveless tops. I'd assumed that Senjogahara was the kind of girl who disapproved of following such trends, but that didn't seem to be the case. She was apolitical that way, which was a new discovery for me. Incidentally, while Hanekawa didn't complain about those kinds of crazes, she didn't partake in them either. Maybe model students differed among themselves depending on whether they were dyed in the wool or not. As far as her skirt went, however, Senjogahara's was still the same length as ever.

She was eating, which meant that her hair in the back and the bangs that she seemed to be growing out lately were tied up with red rubber bands. Some might have found it a stupid-looking hairstyle, but I really enjoyed the way she showed off her neat, pretty forehead, plus it felt good to be able to see her with "her guard down." It was as if she was opening up to me somehow.

"Umm... Huh?" I said, at a loss as to how to react.

"Hmm." Senjogahara used her chopsticks to scoop a bit of white rice out of her lunch box and held it out toward me. "Say ahh."

"........."

Ack!

What...was going on here?!

This was a well-worn scene in manga and the like, something I knew lovey-dovey lovebirds did, but I wasn't happy about it at all! I wanted it to stop, no, I was straight-up scared!

Meanwhile, Senjogahara had on the same flat, expressionless face... I would have been happy to oblige if she'd done it with a bashful, awkward look, but this was one situation where both parties really needed to know how the other felt...

I couldn't help but wonder what she might be planning.

She had to have an ulterior motive.

Maybe ulterior was all there was.

A record with two B-sides.

It might be a feint. Was she planning to laugh at me if I opened my mouth like an idiot?

"What's the matter, Araragi? C'mon, say ahh."

"......"

No...

Why be so mistrustful of your girlfriend?

Senjogahara could be mean, but she'd never do something that horrible. We'd been going out for a month, not what you'd call a long period of time, but long enough to get each other. We'd formed a relationship of trust. What was I thinking, almost destroying it?

I was Senjogahara's boyfriend.

"Ah, aahh," I opened my mouth.

"Take that."

Senjogahara smooshed the rice against my cheek, just right of my opened mouth.

"........."

Hold on, hold on.

True, it was an obvious punch line.

"Heh, heheheh," Senjogahara laughed.

It was a quiet, irritating laugh.

"Heheheh... Ahaha. Haha."

"...I'm delighted to see your smile."

She used to barely ever laugh.

She still only laughed at times like these.

In general, she was just expressionless.

"Araragi, you have rice on your cheek."

"You put it there."

"I'll get it for you," she said, putting down her chopsticks and reaching toward me with her hand. One by one, she carefully picked the grains of rice off from my cheek after having smeared them there herself.

Hmm.

This wasn't bad...

"Okay, it's gone," she said before tossing the clump of rice into a nearby trashcan.

She'd just throw it away? As I watched, too...

Well, not like I thought she'd eat it, of course.

"All right," Senjogahara briskly started over again.

Like she was pretending that nothing had happened.

"I'll go on a date," she repeated.

But then, for some reason, she started to look worried. *Ehh,* she tilted her head as she considered something.

"No, that's not it. A date..."

"...?"

"Could I…bother you for a date?"

"………"

"What would you…think to…about a…date…"

"…………"

Wait a second!

Did she really not know how to make a request?!

I was shocked.

Well, something else was an even bigger shock—Senjogahara had been the one to propose a date, and she'd been so decisive and sudden about it.

Speaking of having gone out with her for a month.

Over that time, I'd openly, and at times even boldly asked her on dates, and she never so much as budged. And yet… Hitagi Senjogahara, she as still as dawn, still as midmorning, still as afternoon, and still as night…was asking for a date?

We had been firm, as if we had signed a pact of silence, in keeping our relationship a "Platonic" one, as my junior Suruga Kanbaru would say. Now we were finally going to go on a date?

What change of mind was this?

As with the "Say ahh" just now, could it be some sort of trap? It was pretty questionable of me to be feeling so paranoid about an offer to go on a date, when she was my girlfriend according to both of us, but that was how shocking it was.

"What," Senjogahara said flatly. "Do you not want to?"

"No, I do, but…"

"By the way, I heard." Senjogahara turned on me a dauntless look that usually isn't meant for your boyfriend. "It sounds like you had quite a bit of fun on your date with Kanbaru. I hear the two of you got intimate and ended up spending last night together?"

"Oh…so you mean you heard from Kanbaru?"

"Yes…though she was quite tight-lipped."

"………"

Why go acting like she had something to hide?!

Flap your lips, because we didn't do anything at all! Keeping it a secret made it seem like something did! Man, people with semi-tight lips were the worst troublemakers!

"She begged me not to blame you."

"Why's she covering for me?! We didn't do anything!"

I'm innocent!

Not guilty!

Falsely accused!

"In any case," Senjogahara said. "I'm glad the two of you seem to be getting along."

"......"

What—was that supposed to mean?

Sure.

Senjogahara probably felt indebted or bad toward Kanbaru—and also knew that Kanbaru and I were rivals in love over none other than Senjogahara herself. So it wasn't exactly incomprehensible that she might feel that way about Kanbaru and me getting along—but there seemed to be some other nuance to her words.

It reminded me of what Hanekawa had told me the day before.

I think that when Senjogahara sees that side of you, it makes her pretty insecure—

The other nuance to her words—

This woman.

What could she be thinking?

"So now," she said, "Kanbaru is worth something to you if she were taken hostage."

"She was thinking of something heinous!"

Hostage?!

Did she just use the word "hostage" in a regular conversation?!

"Kanbaru is so cute, isn't she..." she continued. "And, you know, that cute girl is more than happy to obey my every word. How does that make you feel? Completely as a side note, wouldn't you love to see such a cute girl walking around school on all fours, naked only from the waist down?"

Senjogahara let the hostile line loose with a sigh and an air of forced gloom. Having been born and raised in a peaceful country, I'd never imagined that a threat could wrap itself in such still and nonviolent mannerisms…

Hitagi Senjogahara.

You've just proved that you're no *tsundere*, you're an awful person, that's all…

"How rude, Araragi. That's the first time anyone ever said that about me."

"Really?"

"If anything, people often tell me the opposite. 'What a lovely personality…'"

"They're being sarcastic!"

Hell, if she was okay with it, I'd gladly say it!

What a lovely personality you've got!

"Excuse me? Are you saying those people were being dishonest with me? I won't stand for anyone, even you, Araragi, casting doubts on their words!"

"You're sticking up for people who're insulting you, dammit!"

And so on.

We were just kidding with these conversations.

We were testing each other's wit.

"All right," Senjogahara started over yet again, though the lead-in wasn't remotely all right. "You'll go on a date. With me."

"So that's what you're going to settle on…"

It wasn't too inappropriate a way to phrase it.

In fact, no way to phrase it could be more her.

"Any complaints…I mean, questions?" she followed up.

"No, ma'am…"

Then I'll give whatever excuse and head home early after school, so come pick me up once you're done preparing for the culture festival, please— Senjogahara summarized before returning to her meal as though nothing had happened.

It was very much like her to prioritize our date and skip the culture festival prep as a matter of course, but I certainly wasn't unhappy about getting to go on a date with her. What's more, it would be a nighttime date, a detail with profound implications. As far as where we would go and what we would do, Senjogahara said to leave all the planning to her.

I didn't see any particular reason to object, so I simply decided to look forward to what was to come and mentally pumped my fist.

What a long journey it had been...

Getting my girlfriend to go on a date requiring so much effort was unexpected... I'd overshot and gone on one with her junior Kanbaru beforehand, but all's well that ends well.

In any case.

June thirteenth was going to be a memorable day for me, that of my first date.

However.

A few hours later.

As I made to head home after school once the culture festival prep was done, I found Nadeko Sengoku, my younger sister's old friend, waiting for me outside and was handed volleyball shorts and a school swimsuit; spotted by Hanekawa, I earnestly pled to her, "Please! I'll pay you fifty thousand yen, so don't tell anyone about this!" (Of course, she gave me a serious talking-to in response: "People are endowed with dignity, and you should be ashamed of trying to buy one off." There I stood, holding volleyball shorts and a school swimsuit in my hands, scolded by a classmate by the front gates) before pedaling a little faster than usual on my bicycle to get home, where I changed from my uniform into something more appropriate and doubled back toward Senjogahara's place with nothing more than my wallet and cell phone with me.

It was past 7:30 when I arrived.

I wondered if I was a little late, but Senjogahara greeted me with a "You got here sooner than I expected," followed by a "That's fine, though." It seemed like getting there too early could have been a problem.

Senjogahara had changed out of her school uniform, too.

She had her hair in two bunches in the back. It was a personal rule for her to wear her hair straight down when she was at school, aside from when she ate and during P.E. (which she'd recently started not to skip), and to tie up her hair when she wasn't. Wearing it in two bunches, she took on a vague similarity to Class President Hanekawa, but it did seem like a movement-friendly and stylish choice.

I thought her clothes made it look like we were going to go somewhere, and just as I expected, she said, "Okay, let's go. Follow along now."

But that was as far as my expectations took me.

Some unexpected twists and turns were in store.

Hitagi Senjogahara led me to a jeep parked outside of the Tamikura Apartments, where she lived.

We traveled by car.

That much was fine.

I lived in a motorized society. I had no questions or complaints about that.

The issue was that both Senjogahara and I were strictly forbidden by our school rules to acquire a driver's license. We weren't allowed so much as a scooter, to say nothing of cars. So it followed that both Senjogahara and I got into the jeep's back seats.

So then, who was driving?

Hitagi Senjogahara's father.

"..............."

My girlfriend's father was chaperoning us on our first date?

A date that was more like torture...

Memorable, but how...

The mood in the car, no matter how you spun it, was awkward. We exchanged hurried greetings before the jeep departed. Even then, I couldn't bring myself to ask where we were headed. Actually, our destination didn't even matter to me anymore.

This was, of course, my first time meeting Daddy Senjogahara.

It would be one thing if he were open and sociable, but I had the hardest time dealing with his type, which you might guess, even if I didn't bring up Sengoku, is the silent sort. It was one thing to face a taciturn girl who was younger than me, but a man who was my elder? Daddy Senjogahara was dressed sharply like he'd just come back from work—no, as if he was still on the clock, and quietly operated the steering wheel. He worked at a foreign-owned company or something...

He looked like a stern man. My paranoia was acting up like never before, but it felt like he might get angry at me for just about any reason.

Still…if you put all that aside, while he did look to be on the older side for a father of someone around my age, he cut a pretty cool figure with his full head of salt-and-pepper hair. Like he was an actor. He was "aging gracefully." At the risk of sounding like a doting lover, Hitagi Senjogahara was enough of a beauty that some called her a cloistered princess. But it made sense now, girls like her had fathers like him.

Hmm.

Your father cutting a cool figure netted more points than doing so yourself…

"What's the matter, Araragi?" Senjogahara, who was sitting next to me, asked after we'd driven for a while. "You're awfully quiet."

"Hey… Do you not understand the predicament I'm in right now?"

"I sure don't. When is 'now'? How do you spell 'predicament'?"

"You don't even understand that?!"

Look at her, playing stupid like that.

Did she have no compassion?

"Araragi," she said, "I don't blame you for feeling nervous on our first date, but you need to relax. The night is long."

"Yeah…"

It wasn't because this was our first date…

I truly missed that epoch in my life when I believed a nighttime date had profound implications. I was happy back then. The fact that the night is long was quite simply terrifying. Why did the night have to be long? All I wanted was for it to end as soon as possible…

"Hey, Araragi," Senjogahara said in her flat tone.

She didn't sound nervous at all…

"Do you love me?"

"……!"

What a way to harass someone!

So not only did she have an acid tongue, she was capable of this, too?!

"Answer me. Do you love me?"

"……"

"What's wrong? You're not going to answer me? Hold on, Araragi, could it be that you don't love me?"

45

This was harassment... Ultimate harassment...

"I-I love you..." I said.

"Oh." Senjogahara didn't even smile. Ultimate expressionlessness... "I love you too, Araragi."

"Well...thank you very much."

"Not at all."

...Wait a sec.

So she was unfazed by this?

Totally unfazed that she was having this conversation in front of her real-life father? No, never mind. If it meant being able to harass me, she didn't mind taking collateral damage.

In which case, I thought, furtively casting a sidelong glance at the driver's seat (too furtively for head-on to even be an option). Senjogahara's father, however, had barely reacted. Driving occupied his full attention. What a cool guy... Our jeep seemed to be driving toward the highway. Highway... Were we headed somewhere far? Well, if we weren't, not even Senjogahara would bring her father along on our date, I wanted to think...

Ten minutes later, the jeep did get on the highway. There was no escaping now. Not that I had any thoughts of escaping to begin with, really.

"You're awfully quiet, Araragi. You've hardly opened your mouth, when you're always so voluble. Are you in a sucky mood today?"

"Forget my mood..."

"Oh. Your IQ's what's sucky."

"You couldn't resist taking advantage of my confusion, could you?!"

"You're as spry as ever with the comebacks, at least. Fine, then. As an act of kindness, I'll introduce a topic of conversation myself. All you need to do is reply," Senjogahara said. "What about me do you love?"

"I definitely know what about you I don't love!"

What was she up to?

In fact, it felt like this entire date was a grand harassment plot designed to pit me.

I was starting to want to escape.

"Damn..." I muttered. "And I was actually looking forward to this… It almost felt like a dream come true!"

"Dream? Oh, don't exaggerate," Senjogahara said blankly. "You know, there's no 'm-e' in 'drea'… Wait, how did that go again?"

"Right now I'm wishing there was no 'I'…"

Both were in "nightmare," of course.

Thus a new saying was born.

"Araragi, I can tell that you're suffering… It's so vexing that all I can do is cheer you on from the sidelines."

"No, you know what, I think you can also apologize…"

But.

An apology wasn't going to do anything for me.

If apologies were all it took, who needed the police?

"And I'm not suffering," I said, "so much as feeling very, very exhausted."

"U V-W-X."

"Wha? Oh, I see…"

I wasn't in the mood to laugh for her, though.

There was no room in my heart for it.

At any rate.

"Hey, Senjogahara… Seriously, what do you think you're doing?"

"Senjogahara? Are you referring to me when you say that, or to my dad?"

"………"

This woman… If it's the last thing I do—

No, I needed to calm down. Giving voice to my thoughts now meant a breakup for sure…

"Araragi has something to say to you, Dad."

"Miss Hitagi! I have something to say to you, Miss Hitagi!"

I dared not address her any more casually.

Miss Hitagi.

Just the other day, Kanbaru and I had this same moment where we decided to call each other by our first names. Who could have guessed that the same scene would play itself out like this with my actual girlfriend?

"What could it be, Araragi?"

47

"......"

You're not going to say mine back?

Not that I cared.

"So, Miss Hitagi. I'll ask you once again... Tell me. What do you think you're doing? What are you planning?"

"I'm not planning anything. Anyway, Araragi. You know the famous mystery writer Agatha Christie, don't you? If you rearrange the letters in her name, you get 'a hag is theatric.' Do you think that was on purpose?"

"Who cares about that! If anyone's a theatric hag, it's you!"

"I can't believe you'd say that about me in front of my parent."

"Urk..."

It was a trap!

I fell right into it!

"Dad, it seems like your daughter is a theatric hag."

And now she was reporting it to him...

Daddy Senjogahara still didn't react.

Perhaps he was used to this kind of act from his theatric hag. Yes, now that I thought about it, she was his daughter...

There was no point in getting so upset, then.

She was making me dance like her little monkey, but no song was playing.

"Oh. You've gone quiet again. Did I bully you too much?" she said, looking at me. "You react in such good ways that it makes me want to keep putting you down."

"That line makes me feel more down than anything else you've said yet..."

Honestly.

All right then, I'd try a counterattack.

I wanted to see Senjogahara feeling put down for once.

"So what about me do you love?" I asked.

"How kind you are. How cute you are. How you're like my prince who comes dashing in to save me whenever I'm in trouble."

"My bad!"

Why did I ever think I could fight back?

This wicked woman didn't just have a leg up on me when it came to this, she had a mannequin factory's worth of legs up on me. Why try to fight her ill will with ill will?

Senjogahara was calmness personified.

Did she have no emotions?

Meanwhile, even though I knew that her reply was just a riposte to my harassment, my heart was hammering…

"I don't understand… Why… Where did I go wrong to be walking down this path of thorns…"

"What's wrong with a path of thorns? Elegantly walking down a path filled with roses in bloom is such a gorgeous and beautiful image."

"Don't give it a nice spin!"

"In the language of flowers, roses mean—a foolish man."

"Liar! Stop making stuff up just because you feel like it!"

"By the way," Senjogahara said. She hopped between subjects as she pleased. "By the way, you garba…sorry, Araragi."

"Did you nearly call your own boyfriend 'garbage'?"

"What are you talking about? I wish you wouldn't make such groundless accusations. Anyway, how did you do on the skills test the other day?"

"Hunh?"

"You remember how I minded you, at my home, the two of us alone, day and night?"

"………"

Why phrase it that way…

Why bring up being at her place in her father's absence in front of the man himself?

"All the tests came back last weekend," she said, "but you've avoided talking about it. I assumed that meant your results were absolutely miserable, so I pretended not to care, but I asked Hanekawa today and it sounds like you didn't do so bad?"

"Hanekawa?"

"She's tight-lipped, so of course I couldn't get out the particulars, but she'd tell me if you actually failed."

"………"

Senjogahara must have asked in some awful way.

When Hanekawa turned the talk to Senjogahara in front of the school gates, I did think it was a bit unnatural, but now it made sense. That was the background.

I'd told Hanekawa about my skills test results at the bookstore yesterday... But regardless of Senjogahara's phrasing, I probably was being a bit ungrateful not to speak a word of it to her after all she'd done. I'd somehow demurred thanks to the university issue, which I'd also discussed with Hanekawa.

"Why are you being so reluctant?" she pressed. "Now hurry up and give me the exact scores. If you put on airs, then I'll bend every joint in your body backwards until you paradoxically look kind of cool."

"It won't look cool, in any way!"

"It would look uncool?"

"'Uncool' doesn't begin to describe it!"

"It would look 'lol'?"

"It'd be no laughing matter!"

"So hurry up and tell me if you don't want to walk around in a back bridge for the rest of your life."

"If I had every joint in my body bent backwards, I'd be even worse off!"

I would die.

I would die about five times over before she was done.

"But yeah, I should have told you earlier. Sorry, okay? I did better than I thought. Even at math, which I was always strongest in. It's all thanks to you. Thank you, Senjogahara."

"Dad, Araragi is thanking you about something, won't you listen?"

"Thank you, Miss Hitagi!"

Holy mackeroo.

In any case, I gave her my detailed scores for our six courses in five subjects. Nodding *uh huh*, she had me tell her which questions I got wrong, what I didn't understand, and so on... I was a little surprised to realize that she seemed to remember every question on the tests we took. Then again, she was gifted enough to get the seventh highest score in our school year even while fussing over me...so maybe my surprise was misplaced.

We were finally having something resembling a regular conversation between students.

I could relax a little, even in front of Daddy Senjogahara.

This was my chance to come across as a serious guy.

"It's best, though," remarked Senjogahara, "if we compared answers immediately after a test. But maybe it's unfair to you to demand that much so soon... Anyway, you got decent scores. That's a little unexpected, even if I instructed you myself."

"Unexpected, huh?"

"Yes. It's such an unfunny punch line for you."

"I didn't have you teach me for the laffs!"

"I was looking forward to a development like, 'He studied so hard but ended up doing worse than usual!' I'm disappointed in a way."

"And you don't think looking forward to such a development is unfair to me?!"

"Is that so."

With those words.

Senjogahara plopped her hand down on my leg.

Around my thigh.

......

What was she trying to pull?

By the by, the car we were in may have been a jeep, but it wasn't that big. The two of us were actually pretty close to each other as we both sat in the back...enough so that our bodies touched when the car turned a corner.

Be that as it may, I didn't know how to respond to her going out of her way to touch my thigh...

"Well, that was impressive," she said. "You did a good job."

As if her right hand's movement were completely outside her jurisdiction, Senjogahara advanced the conversation without batting an eye. Why didn't her expression ever change? I had to wonder if she was wearing a well-crafted mask.

"I rarely tell people they did a good job. I wonder how many times I've told people that in the past? You know, I might not have since sixth grade, when this classmate who sat next to me won three times in a row at Reversi."

"That's ages ago, and it's not that impressive!"

"I lied."

"Well, I figured…"

"But it's true that I rarely praise people."

"Yeah…I believe you."

"Of course in this case, I'm only telling myself that I did a good job in a roundabout way. I'm terribly proud that my sage advice bettered a dummy like you, Araragi."

"……"

Well.

That was also technically true.

"If I do say so myself," she added, "how did I ever manage to better a dummy like you who used to spell 'mandrill' as 'man drill'?"

"I've never made that mistake in my life!"

"And it seems like a lot of your wrong answers were due to careless mistakes… Hmm. At this rate, Araragi, you may be able to aim even higher."

"Even higher—you say."

College entrance exams.

Post-graduation options.

"Araragi, I don't mind continuing to help you study as long as that's what you want."

"I couldn't—"

Realistically speaking.

I was still nowhere near the stage where I could tell Senjogahara that I was considering the national university she hoped to get a recommendation to—but that didn't mean I had any reason to turn down her offer.

"—hope for anything more."

"Is that so," Senjogahara said with her composed expression, and nothing more.

A thought ran through my head.

Hanekawa was tight-lipped, plus I had made her promise up, down, and sideways not to tell. There was no way she'd let Senjogahara know about my intentions, but maybe this woman had figured them out anyway.

That would be that. Even if she did know, she seemed ready to wait until I told her myself—

It was like we could communicate wordlessly, which felt good.

"……"

More importantly, not satisfied with touching my thigh, Senjogahara started to caress it, working all the way to my inner thigh. What could it mean?

Wasn't this like groping?

Is it something you did in front of your father?

…Well, behind your father, to be precise.

"In that case," she said, "you'll be studying at my place every day."

"E-Every day?!"

I never wordlessly communicated that to her!

Wait, hold on…

Could that be how much I needed to study? But every day… Every single one? I did study during classes, didn't I? Was I going to have to after school and on Sundays as well?

"What? Is something the matter, Araragi?"

"W-Well…I was just thinking that I guess smart people do study that much."

"Nope. I don't, it'd be a pain. It's a program designed for you, who else."

"………"

A natural…

She with the seventh best grades in my year just told me that studying was a pain…

"Smart people are smart from before they study," she said. "Grades only measure your ability to digest and memorize."

"Huh… Oh, but what about Hanekawa? She said she comes down with a headache if she doesn't study, or something."

"What she means by 'study,' Araragi, is sadly on a different level from what we mean by it." Senjogahara paused before continuing,

"Hanekawa is the real deal. She exists in a different world than the one you and I live in."

"...Huh."

So—even Senjogahara saw her that way.

So there was a divide.

Seventh in our year, and first in our year.

Both in the single digits, but a difference that vast existed.

"The real deal, huh?"

"Maybe more. Unreal, or 'monster'—might be a better way to put it. I mean, doesn't it creep you out? When someone is that sharp, we're no longer talking about wits."

Senjogahara's usual venom—

This didn't sound like it.

She was always this way, somehow, when it came to Hanekawa.

It wasn't antipathy, but—

She did maintain an odd distance.

"Did you just say 'you and I'?"

"Yes," replied Senjogahara. "You and me both. Just as Hanekawa and I might look similar to you—I think she looks at you and me as being on the same level."

"Really?"

"Really. It's highly humiliating."

"Oh, so that's humiliating..."

Highly, too.

She really did like putting me down, didn't she?

"Still," I said, "it's not like Hanekawa always gets perfect scores, right? Well, I guess she almost always gets perfect scores..."

"When Hanekawa doesn't get a perfect score, it's because a test question was flawed... I don't know, though. When I think about how much pressure that must put on her...I can't honestly say that I'm jealous."

"Pressure, huh?"

"Or maybe stress."

"Stress."

Tsubasa Hanekawa.

A girl with a pair of mismatched wings—

"At the same time, we'd be wrongheaded to commiserate with her on that account." *In any case,* Senjogahara brought our conversation back on point. "Araragi, you who're crawling and writhing at the bottom, far from the real deal, just need to grind it out. So. You're studying at my place every day."

"Yes, yes…I will."

"You need to say 'yes' three times, Araragi."

"Yes, yes, yes! …Wait, why do you want me to sound so excited?!"

"That's just how much motivation I want to be seeing from you. Because I'm offering my home to you as a study spot."

"You are?"

"If you prefer, I could come to yours."

"My place isn't a very good study environment… My little sisters are loud."

"Kanbaru's house might work out, too, from time to time."

"Why are you bringing her up now?"

"Just as I have to help you study, I need to go and play with that kid once in a while. I promised her," Senjogahara said, her tone markedly flat.

I could tell that the flatness was marked.

With me, she was an awful person through and through, but at least you could honestly call her a tsundere when it came to Kanbaru…

Well, to the hostage.

Suruga Kanbaru.

"The kid seems to be doing fine in the academic department," Senjogahara said, "but am I the only one who wants to hang around with Kanbaru?"

"Well, sure. She's fun."

A little too fun.

Not to mention.

"She admires me in this excessive way, and I don't even know why… I think she sees me in too good of a light."

"I may be partially responsible for that," Senjogahara explained. "I did tell her that you saved a drowning child and that you spend every Sunday volunteering at a retirement home."

"So you've told her nothing but lies!"

"Just kidding. I told her the plain truth."

"Huh…really?"

"When I say the plain truth, I mean badmouthing you, so Kanbaru admiring you is entirely her own decision."

"…………"

Badmouthing me, eh?

I'd rather you didn't, Senjogahara.

"Even if I'm talking to a junior and a friend," she said, "it's embarrassing for me to praise my own boyfriend. It's my way of hiding my feelings."

"Well, you could also just tell her you feel embarrassed… Oh, that's right, Senjogahara." Lowering my voice so her father in the driver's seat wouldn't hear, I brought up a new topic. "There's one more thing about Kanbaru…"

"Dad? Araragi wants to tell you a secret—"

"Miss Hitagi!"

God, she never missed a thing!

She never let an opportunity to torment me get by her!

"What about Kanbaru?" she asked.

"Why is she so pervy?"

I spoke concealing my mouth with my hand.

It was like I was a pitcher trying to communicate with my catcher, but I had no choice because Daddy Senjogahara might read my lips in the rearview mirror.

"Pervy? Kanbaru?"

"Yeah. Was she like that in junior high, too?"

"Hmm. You're asking about the past…but is she, to begin with?"

"You'd say otherwise? Even Oshino sees her as a pervy rather than sporty character."

"I don't know about that. Maybe it's only from a male perspective that seeks chastity in women that she looks that way to you and Mister Oshino? It's guy thinking. She's simply true to herself, that's all. I don't think she ever goes too far."

"I see…"

56

Is that how it was?

I wasn't sure.

"If you have a chance, Araragi, try reading boys' love novels and manga for middle school girls and up. You'd never call someone like Kanbaru 'pervy' again."

"Okay… Uh, I don't think I'll actually read any, though."

Especially not BL fiction.

I'd be doomed, for good.

"Fine," Senjogahara said. "But I can't allow myself to sit back and let my adorable little junior get maligned as a perv."

"What exactly are you going to do, then?"

And malign?

I actually saw myself as a sort of victim… This wasn't working. Senjogahara was going to side with Kanbaru unconditionally and unlimitedly no matter how long we discussed her.

A hostage though she was…

Hold on, wasn't I the hostage here?

"You want to know what I'm going to do? I'm going to undermine your standards and values. That way, you'll start to see Kanbaru as a positively innocent girl," Senjogahara said, leaning toward me.

Instead of just lowering her voice, she brought her lips right next to my ear, as if to conspire openly.

Cupping her hand over her mouth.

"—#@&$."

"……!"

Gah!

What did she just say to me?!

"I'll @&~* that $&#~ into #&@~ so #&—and *@ with #&^&—~&@ in @&—"

"U…urk!"

Hitagi Senjogahara…

Wh-What an embarrassing, indecent thing to say!

~&@ in @&?!

Of all the combinations, that?!

And she was saying it all in such a flat, businesslike voice!

I couldn't believe it…how could a guy find his passions so ignited by nothing more than words?!

"S-Sto—"

Ack… No, I couldn't yell!

Daddy Senjogahara was right in front of me!

I had to seem natural!

"^#~—and $&# while @%%—"

"Nkk…"

B-But the faint tickle I felt on my ear on top of it from her breathing… Hold on, what was this situation?! My girlfriend was caressing my thigh and whispering dirty things into my ear—in front of her own father! This wasn't practically torture, it was literally torture! What did I have to confess to in order to make it stop?!

I don't know anything!

Really, I don't!

I see…I see it now, mystery solved—you were Kanbaru's master in the ways of perversion all along! All I needed to do was think about it, given how much of an influence her senior, Senjogahara, once had on her… Dammit, my standards and values were being undermined and were collapsing… Ah, Kanbaru isn't pervy, she isn't a perv at all…

"Haumph."

She bit my ear!

Like, between her lips!

No, no, no! Now she was doing something unmistakably erotic!

"So like that," Senjogahara said, backing away as though nothing had happened, calm and collected. "What do you think, Araragi?"

"Have your way with me…Miss Hitagi."

I was no good anymore.

This was, in no way, the date that I'd wanted to go on… My hopes, dreams, and fantasies—she really was going through them and smashing them one by one…

Time had flown all the while.

We'd gotten off the highway, I noticed. As far as I could tell from looking out the window, we were in an even more rural area than the remote town we lived in.

Where was I?

Where had they taken me?

While I was having a stupid conversation...

"We're almost there," Senjogahara said, likewise looking out the window. "About thirty more minutes—I think? The timing seems...just right. I feel like complimenting myself."

Whatever was just right, shouldn't the credit for anything time-related go to Daddy Senjogahara, and wasn't she going to thank him?

Hmm.

Maybe they didn't get along very well.

Speaking of which, Senjogahara and Daddy Senjogahara hadn't really exchanged words apart from a simple back-and-forth before our departure.

But—they couldn't be on bad terms. She'd raised Oshino's hundred-thousand-yen fee for his assistance with her aberration by helping out at her father's job.

Well.

Parent-child relationships were going to be complicated at our age—it was the same for me, and Senjogahara had unusual family circumstances to deal with, too.

Even Hanekawa.

......

Oh, now I remembered.

Hanekawa's headache... It'd gotten lost in the brouhaha over the volleyball shorts and school swimsuit, but... (and I didn't know about it getting lost over that, but...) Her headache.

Her head ached.

I wondered if I should talk to Oshino.

True, it wasn't good for me to be so quick to rely on Oshino—just as he'd told me, it wasn't as if he was going to be living in that abandoned building forever—

One day he would leave.

I didn't know when, but in the near future.

"Hey, Senjo—Miss Hitagi."

"Silence." Rather than applauding me for noticing halfway through and correcting myself, Senjogahara smacked me down. "You just keep going on about this, that, and the otter."

"O-Otter?"

"We're almost there, so try staying quiet for at least a small bit of this trip?"

"......"

Where was this coming from...

"Araragi, I'm neither the kind of idler or fiddler who would bother putting up with your idiotic talk."

"So you're saying a fiddler would?"

And where were we almost?

It didn't seem like it would hurt if she told me already.

If she wasn't telling so that I'd be excited, I hoped she knew that I'd already had my fill of excitement.

But while I say that, I was also starting to reach the end of my rope when it came to this torture chat in front of Senjogahara's father. In a sense, her words were exactly what I wanted to hear. *Got it,* I slumped into my seat.

"Ugh, you're so loud."

"What? But I didn't say anything?"

"I'm talking about your breathing and your heartbeat."

"Hold on, what you're doing is telling me to die."

And with that exchange.

Senjogahara stopped talking, too.

I wondered why.

She was nervous for some reason—or at least it looked that way.

Was she taking me somewhere worth being nervous about?

Our car seemed to be going up a mountain road.

A mountain—and not a small mountain like the one I had climbed with Kanbaru yesterday and the day before, but a full-blown mountain. The jeep made use of its horsepower as it climbed the large, spiraling path. The road was properly maintained, another difference from the earlier mountain.

Were we headed for the summit?

Another shrine?

A shrine visit as our first date…

She had to be kidding.

"I feel like I'm asking this too late," I said, "but…where exactly are we going?"

"Somewhere really nice."

"……"

"Somewhere. Really. Nice."

"………"

She could say it seductively all she wanted…

She had to be lying.

"And anyway, Araragi, forget about where we're going. We've already arrived. Look, right over there. That's the parking lot."

I did as she said and looked ahead. She was right.

We arrived.

It was now close to ten…which meant we'd been on the road for over two hours. It was a breathtakingly terrifying trip, and I was able to at last take a regular breath. Daddy Senjogahara displayed some impressive parking technique to stop the jeep in the corner of the deserted parking lot. *Sheesh,* I thought as I tried to get out of the car, but Senjogahara stopped me. She didn't stop me by grabbing my hand, but astonishingly, by stabbing her fingernails into the thigh she'd been rubbing.

What was she, a wild animal?

Or some cat?

"Y-Yes?"

"You wait here a second, Araragi," Senjogahara said. "I'm going to go by myself first and get ready."

"Get ready…"

It involved getting ready?

And wait, Senjogahara, if you go ahead on your own in this situation and make me wait here—

"You have a friendly little chat with my dad, okay?" she uttered the unthinkable words in a throwaway tone.

Then she really got out of the jeep alone.

She was gone…

I never thought the day would come when I'd describe myself in this way, but there was no better way to put it…I felt like a dog that had been abandoned by its master.

I couldn't believe her.

Leaving me in this predicament…

I felt crossed and double-crossed.

Even crisscrossed!

…I was in such a panic that I didn't know what I was saying to myself anymore.

But this was no betrayal because Hitagi Senjogahara had been dragging me into this predicament from the very beginning.

Even so, I couldn't believe it…

I was stuck in a cramped car with my girlfriend's father…

It wasn't even torture anymore.

I was doing time.

You would search all of Japan in vain for high school seniors going through an experience as cruel and harsh as mine—probably? What a down-to-earth and real misfortune.

A f-friendly little chat?

Keeping my mouth shut felt awkward in its own way…but I didn't want Senjogahara's father to get a bad impression of me. Still…outside of relatives and teachers, I'd barely had any opportunities to speak with someone who was easily twice my age…

Then.

As I sat there hesitating, lo and behold, Daddy Senjogahara was the one who got the ball rolling.

"Araragi—is that your name?"

"……"

That was my name…

It felt like he was starting the bar high…

He really did have a nice voice, though, like an actor… It's surprisingly rare to meet someone whose voice strikes you as cool.

"Y-Yes…my name is Koyomi Araragi," I replied.

"I see." Daddy Senjogahara nodded. "Take good care of my daughter from now on."

Excuse me?!

What was this dude saying all of sudden?!

"Just kidding."

That's how he continued.

…Just kidding…

A dad joke?

Was it an authentic dad joke?!

He'd spoken without so much as a smile—and didn't seem to be getting a kick out of my bafflement… What was I supposed to do? There was nothing I could do, was there?

"I think you've heard already, Araragi—but I'm like the very definition of a workaholic. I barely get to spend any time with Hitagi."

"Right…"

Hitagi, he said.

Naturally, he called his daughter by her first name.

He made it sound so natural, too.

I guess that's what it meant to be someone's parent.

"So this might not sound very convincing coming from me—but it's been a long time since I last saw Hitagi having this much fun."

"……"

Did he understand what he was saying? He was describing his daughter tormenting a classmate as "having fun"?

Ah, er, Daddy Senjogahara tread water at that point. It seemed that he wasn't as eloquent as his daughter—if anything, he was a fairly poor speaker.

"You've already heard about Hitagi's mother, yes?"

"…Yes."

"Which means you've heard about her illness, too."

Hitagi Senjogahara's illness—he called it an illness, but he was referring to that aberration.

The crab.

The crab—aberration.

The illness had already been cured, thanks to Oshino's help—but it wasn't so minor an issue that getting cured meant it was over and done with.

Especially from her family's point of view, I assumed.

"It's not the only reason—I'm in no small part to blame for focusing on nothing but my work…but Hitagi really closed off her heart."

"Yes—I know that."

I knew that well.

We'd been in the same class throughout high school.

My first and second years.

The first month of my third year.

I knew very well—just how closed-off her heart had been.

"I don't have any excuse for it—parents might be responsible for what their children do, but children don't bear any responsibility for what their parents do."

"Responsibility…"

"When you close off your heart, there are only two categories of people to whom you speak your mind: people you don't mind being hated by—and people who won't hate you."

"……"

When I first came in contact with Senjogahara and she brandished that stapler at me—she had to have seen me as belonging to the former of the two. She threw off her mask of the cloistered princess and revealed her true and terrifying nature to me only because I was an enemy who had learned her secret.

But now?

Did she really put that much trust in me? Even if she did, was I qualified to receive it?

"There's everything that happened with her mother. And—the illness, too," Daddy Senjogahara said as though to himself. "She's someone whose nature it is to love—she just doesn't know how."

He wasn't saying anything outlandish when I thought about it, but I felt like I'd been treated to an incredibly poetic remark thanks to his cool voice.

"Araragi, I think you're handling someone like Hitagi very well."

"You think so?"

I did feel hurt each time, okay?

Like I was getting sliced up, okay?

If my figurative heart could bleed, I'd have died long ago of massive blood loss.

"She's always like that," I said. "I'm even wondering if it was just to find ways to put me down that she made you accompany us, Dad."

Oops.

I accidentally called him Dad...

W-Was I going to hear it now? That legendary phrase, "You'll never call me Dad"?!

"I doubt it."

He didn't say it.

A generational thing?

"Well, it might be her way of spiting me," he suggested instead.

"Spiting?"

...Huh?

Oh—right.

His daughter flirting with a boy he'd never met before in the backseat of his own car couldn't have been pleasant—obviously. That was the exact reason why I couldn't take it anymore, but had she been trying to harass her father that way, more so than me?

"No," I disagreed, "I don't think that's true... Even, uh, Miss Hitagi, wouldn't do that to you..."

"Someone she doesn't mind being hated by—I'm one of them," Daddy Senjogahara said. "Whether or not she succeeds, I'm still her father. She did see me in a lot of ugly arguments with her mother... By now, Hitagi probably can't recall her parents ever getting along."

"Ah—"

An uncontested divorce.

A single-father home.

Of course.

All this time, he never said "wife," and every time—it was "Hitagi's mother."

"So yes—spite. I could practically hear Hitagi saying that she'd never become like us. In fact—I think she's right. You two honestly looked like you were having fun."

"Well... I'd be lying if I said I wasn't having any fun at all, but...I don't know, I'm used to her acting like a total nutjob."

Wait.

Was that an impolite thing to say?

What if he took it at face value and heard it as an insult? I thought I was almost praising her, but friendly trash talk could be interpreted negatively on the receiving end, depending on the occasion... Hmm, I didn't know where to draw the line.

Hold on, why all this solo wrestling?

Was I being, like, incredibly lame?

"She's someone whose nature it is to love," Daddy Senjogahara said, "so she leans in and gives all of herself over when she finds the right person. To love is to demand. I know this is my own daughter I'm talking about here, but I think she's too heavy of a burden to be called a girlfriend."

"Too heavy—of a burden."

That, there.

How ironic.

"Though I couldn't be any more ashamed of the fact, I wasn't able to support Hitagi. That's why she stopped depending on me a long time ago."

"………"

"I forget when, but she went on a rampage swinging a stapler... I think that was the last time."

She'd even done that to her father.

Was that domestic violence or...

"But the other day—for the first time in a while, a long, long while, Hitagi asked me for something. She said—she wanted to help me with my work," Daddy Senjogahara said in quiet contemplation. "And now, this. Both times—you've been involved. I think you're something special if you're able to cause a change in that girl."

"...I'm flattered that you think so highly of me, but...I think it's all just coincidence," I said at last, unable to take it any longer. It felt like I was being praised due to a misunderstanding. I hadn't earned it, and to be honest, it wasn't a good feeling.

"Really? I heard you played a part in curing Hitagi's illness, too."

"Yes, and again—it could've been anyone but just so happened to be me... Anyone else could have taken my place, and Miss Hitagi just got saved on her own to begin with. I ended up being present for it, that's all."

"That's enough. The simple fact that you were there when she needed you to be is enough. There's nothing more you had to do to earn her gratitude."

And then, for the first time.

I thought I saw Daddy Senjogahara smile.

"I wasn't able to carry out my duties as a father—I still don't think of myself as caring for my daughter. That girl is all but living on her own. I wasn't able to be there when she needed me. My hands are full trying to pay off the debts Hitagi's mother created for us, to be honest—even this jeep is borrowed from a friend. But despite all my failings as a father, I'm still proud of my daughter. I trust her eye for people. And if you're the one she brought, you must be the right one."

"......"

"Take good care of my daughter from now on—Araragi."

"...Dad."

Now this—had become a strange conversation.

Still, I thought.

She probably wasn't trying to spite him.

If anything, Senjogahara might have asked her father to accompany her on her first date because she wanted to show him that she was okay now.

It wasn't to tell him she'd never become like her parents—

Rather, he didn't need to worry about her anymore.

I felt like I could hear her saying it.

...But it wasn't for me to tell him. Not sticking your nose in other people's family environment—there was that common sense, but more so, I felt like there was no space between Senjogahara and Daddy Senjogahara for me.

So it wasn't for me to tell him.

That he wasn't someone she didn't mind being hated by, no matter how I thought about it—but someone who wouldn't hate her.

I couldn't possibly tell him.

There was only one person in the world who should say those words.

"By the way," I asked, "where are we?"

"If Hitagi's keeping it a secret, then I can't tell you. But—we're in a place…that the three of us visited a few times."

"The three of you?"

Meaning…Senjogahara, Daddy Senjogahara, and—

Mommy Senjogahara?

"You know, picking this spot for her first date makes me think she's quite—whoops. It looks like the princess has returned."

What a dad-like way to put it.

That would have been my retort if I were talking to someone my own age, but I exercised restraint.

Anyway, he said Senjogahara had returned…and indeed, through the window I could see her taking her time walking toward us. Ah, until just a moment ago I'd been meaning to gripe at her when I saw her next for abandoning me to my predicament, but now it was as if an angel were descending from heaven to rescue me.

What a con.

"Thanks for waiting, Araragi," she said in an unconcerned and flat voice after opening the back door. She then turned straight to the driver's seat. "Dad, could you give us two youngsters some time alone? Thank you for bringing us here. We should be back in about two hours, so please, do get back to your job."

"Sure," Daddy Senjogahara consented and flashed his cell phone. I'd imagined it to be the case, but he'd agreed to interrupt his busy work schedule to drive us around…and he was getting back to work on his phone.

Hm.

Which meant…his chaperoning ended here?

"Okay, Araragi."

Senjogahara extended her hand toward me. I took it, with fear and trepidation in my heart. I exited the car as if Senjogahara were pulling me out of it.

She let go of my hand a second later.

She really was chaste.

"I appreciate it, Dad."

Finally thanking him, she closed the jeep's door.

Well—not that it meant anything, but...at last we were on a normal date. I felt a little awkward about leaving Daddy Senjogahara in the parking lot when he'd taken us all the way into the mountains on a weekday night, but he seemed to have work he could do, so I let it slide.

"...So, where exactly are we, Miss Hita—"

Oops.

I could drop that now.

I did feel a little reluctant to let it go.

"Senjogahara. Where are we?"

"Hmph." Senjogahara tossed her head. "Have I ever once answered any of your questions?"

"......"

Um.

Yes, I think so?

Senjogahara's attitude toward me that moment was so callous that I began to think that maybe I was one of those people she didn't mind being hated by.

"Asking me a question," she spat. "I think you're getting a big head."

"I'm not even allowed to ask you questions..."

"I don't remember allowing you to so much as kneel."

"I don't want to kneel!"

"You mean you'd rather kowtow?"

"Do you have some kind of issue with me standing?!"

I could quip to my heart's content now that her father was out of the picture.

Koyomi Araragi was firing on all cylinders.

I followed behind Senjogahara as she briskly forged ahead. We may have been in the mountains, but the scattered streetlights in the parking lot meant it wasn't what you'd call dark... Wait, do you still call them streetlights even in the mountains? The inconsequential thought ran through my head.

"I'm glad the weather turned out to be nice, though."

"The weather?" I asked her. "Is that important?"

"Yes."

"Huh… Well, they do call me Mister Sunshine."

"Sorry? Mister Dumb Swine?"

"There's no way you could have misheard me like that!"

"Look," Senjogahara said around the time we left the parking lot. "Do you see the sign over there? Try reading it."

"Hrm?"

Ordering me in such an offhanded, almost sulking way… But I did as Senjogahara said and looked where she was pointing. There was indeed a sign there, and written on it were the words "Home of the Stars Observatory."

An observatory?

In other words…

"Hiya!"

Senjogahara used her right hand to stop my head when I reflexively tried to look up toward the sky. Grabbing my head from above, she kept it in place.

"What are you doing?" I complained.

It was pretty humiliating to have that done to me at my age…

"You can't look up yet, Araragi. You can't look ahead, either. Just look down at your feet as you walk. This is an order."

"I can't follow such an unreasonable order!"

"Well, if you won't, I'll start screaming and crying and run back to that jeep where my dad is waiting."

"……"

"Or maybe Kanbaru will meet a bit of an unfortunate fate tomorrow. Which do you prefer? A high school girl cosplaying a kindergartener, and taking classes—or a high school girl with a sign that says 'I'm being punished because I'm a very slutty girl' hanging from her neck, and standing out in the hall?"

"…I'll do it."

You hear about using the carrot and the stick in negotiations, but she was appallingly all stick… Lowering my head instead, I gazed down at my feet. Hitagi Senjogahara didn't let go of my head, though. With her hand still in place, she said, "Shall we?" and began walking again.

Oh god.

I was like a dog being walked.

"…You really are s-scary, you know that?"

"What's the extra 's' for? But think of it as part of my brand of hospitality. I want you to feel a bit scarred."

"And you added an extra 'r'! Listen to you, you say the meanest things! Treat me with some heart!"

"I sure can, with heat."

"That's where you got the spare 'r' from?!"

"Oh, stop whining. It's only polite to add a little espresso to any conversation."

"Too bitter for a high school student's palate…"

Of course, the right word was *esprit*.

It grew dark as soon as we left the parking lot.

Even so—we were by a mountaintop observatory, and I could tell even without looking up that it wasn't pitch-black, thanks to the starlight. We lived in a fairly remote town, which meant we could at least spot the constellations in the sky at night, but it was probably no match to out here.

Oh.

That's when I finally remembered.

"You know, about Kanbaru."

"Yes? Is this concerning her unfortunate fate?"

"Why would I keep on discussing that?!"

"Well said. If she's going to meet an unfortunate fate, you want to decide all the details on your own from A to Z."

"I'm not going to let Kanbaru meet an unfortunate fate at anyone's hands! Even if those hands are yours! That's not what I'm talking about!"

"Then what is it?"

"Kanbaru and I were talking about constellations the other day. Two days ago, I think?"

Ophiuchus.

Going too far into it would touch on Senjogahara's birthday, so I had to keep it simple.

"Kanbaru told me something then," I went on. "She attends these

71

events at an observatory in another prefecture two times a year. Could this be where?"

Senjogahara had influenced Suruga Kanbaru down to their perviness, so it was entirely possible.

"Must be," Senjoghara replied sure enough. "But it's been a while since my last visit… I do remember telling that kid. Hm… So Kanbaru does that."

"She asked if it seemed out of character for her, come to think of it. So that's what she meant. Man, what an adorable little junior she is."

"Yes. So much so that I wanna do her."

"In what sense?!"

Oh… Now I recalled one more thing. That day I first visited Senjogahara's home and told her the whopper about knowing a lot about astronomy…something about what the moon looks like. I remembered sharing my half-assed expertise and Senjogahara turning the tables on me.

Agh, how embarrassing.

I wished the memory had stayed forgotten.

Of course she'd turn the tables on me.

This was the first time I'd ever been to an observatory.

"Looks like there's no one around, though," I said.

"This isn't a particularly good time for observing stars. Plus it's a weekday. Anyone that is here is probably inside that observatory over there."

"Over where?"

I tried to raise my head, to no avail.

Or rather, I felt nails digging into my scalp.

"Hey, Senjogahara… Are you aware that you're definitely doing something a lot meaner than you think right now?"

"Really?" My kind admonition was greeted with total indifference by Hitagi Senjogahara. "If anything, you should feel fortunate to have one of my delicate hands on your head."

"I'll give you that, if you mean delicate like glass…whole shards of it."

"What a wonderful thing to hear. Am I so clear and sharp? You really know how to compliment a girl. I feel like rewarding you."

Her nails dug deeper into my scalp.

It was a simple yet effective way of delivering pain.

Was she actually made of the stuff? Senjogahara's hollow, emotionless eyes were nothing if not glassy, in fact.

I see, so that's what my girlfriend was…

Hitagi Shard.

"Anyway," I asked her, "there's an observatory around here?"

"Yes. With a large reflecting telescope."

"Huh. I don't quite get what's so amazing about that, but…we're going in there?"

"Nope," Senjogahara shook her head right away. "It costs money to enter."

"……"

"I'm poor, I'll have you know."

I didn't see the point in saying it with such pride, but…

I guess it was the truth.

"I don't mind paying," I said, "since an observatory probably doesn't charge too much. I'm sure I have at least that much cash on me."

"I applaud your readiness to take the bill, but I'll have to turn down your offer for today. I have a spot I recommend over looking through a telescope in a building—ah. This way."

Senjogahara left the path to begin climbing a hill. She stepped through the cropped grass, and I followed in her footsteps.

She stopped about halfway up the hill.

A plastic sheet had been placed on the ground there.

Ah, her preparations.

"Close your eyes and lie down."

I didn't feel like opposing or defying her when I'd come this far. Senjogahara's intentions were clear to me now. I did as she said, closing my eyes and lying down on the sheet. Her hand left my head, and I could sense someone lying down next to me. I say "someone," but that'd be some incredible magic trick if it weren't Senjogahara.

"You can open your eyes now."

I did as she said.

And then, the heavens were full of stars.

"..Whoa."

To be honest.

I was surprised less by the beautiful starry sky than by myself for still being able to find a starry sky beautiful at my age.

Humans could feel this moved?

The stars seemed to rain down on us.

If I may be so unrefined, it could have been in part because I was lying down… But it was simply fantastic to have stars covering every inch of my vision. Trying to coddle my self-consciousness by searching for the reason that I was moved was already pretty disingenuous, but I understood why Senjogahara had gone so far as to stick her nails in my head to keep me from taking a sneak peek. She'd wanted me to see this sky from this perspective first.

Somewhere really nice.

She was right. There was nowhere nicer.

Ah… Somehow I felt like I'd been fully repaid.

Like all of the pain and trouble so far was being washed away.

"So, Araragi—what do you think?" Senjogahara asked by my side.

She—must have been looking at the same sky.

"Wow—seriously, I don't have the words for it."

"So your vocabulary is lacking," she said, putting a damper on my emotions with her acid tongue.

But—that was the extent of it.

Even her venom was tempered under this sky.

"There's Deneb. Altair. Vega. The famous Summer Triangle. Go aaaall the way to the side from there, and we get to Ophiuchus. Which means Serpens is those stars in that area."

Senjogahara gave me an eloquent explanation as she pointed at the night sky.

Such fluid commentary, though we were using neither a penlight nor a planisphere.

Somehow, it was easy to understand.

"That conspicuously bright star is Spica…which means Virgo is around there. Cancer is over there… Oh, maybe it's a bit hard to make out."

"I guess I know the Big Dipper."

"Yes, and the Big Dipper is part of Ursa Major—right next to it is Lynx."

"Like the cat?"

"Yes."

Senjogahara continued to name every constellation we could see and to tell me about each one. It was as if I was listening to a fairy tale, and her words seeped into me like a balm.

If she'd let me.

I wanted to drift off to sleep.

"You can't fall asleep," she said.

What a clear no.

What a sharp girl.

She continued, "Or as I'd say if we were mountain climbers stranded in a blizzard—'You can't fall asleep! I'll kill you if you do!'"

"You're doing the killing?!"

"Well, in any case," Senjogahara spoke in a flat voice—having wrapped up her commentary on the constellations. "That's everything."

"Huh? What is?"

"Everything I have," she said, still looking at the stars. "Being able to help you study. My cute little junior and my curt father. And— these stars. That's all I have, really. That's about everything I can give you. That's it, everything."

"Everything…"

Oh…was that the deal?

The thing with Kanbaru the day before yesterday… No, since we first started dating a month ago on Mother's Day, was that what Senjogahara was thinking the whole time? Never betraying any interest when I asked her out on a date… Making up with Kanbaru might have been unplanned, but had she been waiting for our skills test to be over and for her father's schedule to open up?

I remembered something Hanekawa had said—

Senjogahara is a tough one.

"Well, technically speaking," she corrected herself, "I do also have my acid tongue and verbal abuse."

"I don't need that!"

"And I guess I do have this body of mine."

"......"

This body of mine...

Her euphemisms were so naked.

"Do you not need that, either?"

"Er, well... Um."

I—couldn't say no, could I?

But something about the scene made saying yes feel off, too...

"But you know, don't you?" she said. "That a long time ago—a filthy man tried to assault me."

"Oh...yeah."

The crab.

It was—the reason for that aberration.

One reason, at least.

There were reasons for aberrations.

"And frankly, I'm scared of doing with you what that filth tried to do to me. No—I don't intend on using fancy words like 'trauma.' I don't think I'm such a wuss. I'm simply...scared. It wasn't that bad before we started going out—but now, I'm scared of hating you, Araragi."

She was scared.

Not of the act, but of the result.

"Now I'm scared of losing you," Senjogahara said matter-of-factly.

I couldn't read any emotions into her voice.

Her face was probably expressionless, too.

"It's funny, isn't it? Being scared of hating the person you're dating, being scared of losing the person you're dating... It's like which comes first, the egg or the sunny-side up."

"The egg, I think."

"To tell you the truth, I'm afraid I've become a stupid woman. I was supposed to be a tragic, beautiful maiden who suffered from a mysterious, unknown illness—but now I'm a lovestruck, beautiful maiden who's always thinking about some guy."

"So you're a beautiful maiden in either case..."

"Anyway, I even resent you for turning me into such an uninteresting, dime-a-dozen woman."

"Uh huh…"

Nah…you're plenty interesting.

Sorry, I didn't mean to interrupt.

"As you're aware, though, Araragi—I haven't led the happiest life up until now… But I think I could call it all even if I see it as what let me meet you."

"……"

"If it was my unhappiness that caught your attention—then I'm glad it happened that way. That's how taken I am with you. So no matter how small the chance, I don't want to see you in the same light I see that filth. Of course, I don't plan on being this selfish forever… I do feel like I'm being childish. Like I'm being a baby. A naive widdle baby…"

Why repeat it in a lamer way, Senjogahara?

"If you'll allow me a shallow line," she said, "losing you would be like losing half of my own body. So I want you to wait, just a little."

"Just a little—"

"Yes. Until next week."

"So soon?!"

"Please satisfy yourself with Kanbaru's body until then."

"Did you really just say that to me?!"

"And while you do that, I'll use Kanbaru to rehab, too."

"Kanbaru is getting the best of it! Only she gets all of her dreams to come true?"

"Well, next week isn't realistic—but I swear I'll make it work some day. So please, I want you to wait, just a little. As far as what this love-struck woman can give you—these stars are it for now… When I was younger, we used to come here often. My dad, my mom—and me."

With her mom and dad—the three of them together.

I thought about what I knew of her family situation—and realized that must have been quite a while ago. Even so—Senjogahara remembered.

No.

Recalled.

She'd recalled something she'd forgotten.

"This is it. My treasure."

It was a pretty cliché turn of phrase for Senjogahara—but that only added to the sense she was sharing her unadorned, true feelings with me.

This starry summer sky.

This sky she once saw with her family.

This was it—everything.

"....................."

At the very least.

I could say I was now sure of one thing.

Hitagi Senjogahara…was quite smart, and extraordinarily calculating, but she had zero combat ability when it came to romance. It was obvious enough on Mother's Day during the events that led to us going out, but this woman was, how to put it, foolhardy, like an RPG hero who charges into a cave without a torch. She thought showing me all her cards and leaving the decision in my hands, her diplomatic blackmail of a methodology, was a good approach to take to something as subtle as falling in love? Where was the sentiment in that? That come-on was bound to give pause to ninety-nine out of a hundred people. Talk about feeling scared. Even someone as devoid of romantic experience as me knew that much.

Well.

If she was adopting the strategy fully aware that I was the one remaining person in a hundred—then dammit, I had to take my hat off to her.

Uh oh.

So adorable.

So *moé*, it wasn't funny.

I actually felt like riding the momentum and hugging Senjogahara—but didn't want to lose her, either, over such a thing. Not that I had any cards to show her… But I was okay with our relationship being this way for now.

It's not as if I didn't need it, though.

We could lie on our backs and look up at the stars.

We were fine as that sort of couple.

A Platonic relationship.

"Hey, Araragi," Senjogahara deadpanned. "Do you love me?"

"I do."

"I do, too. I love you, Araragi."

"Thank you."

"What about me do you love?"

"Everything. There's nothing about you that I don't love."

"Oh. I'm happy to hear that."

"And what do you love about me?"

"You're kind. You're cute. You're like my prince who comes dashing in to save me when I'm in trouble."

"I'm happy to hear that."

"By the way," Senjogahara said as if she'd just realized, "that filth was only after my body—he didn't even try to steal my lips."

"Huh? What do you mean?"

"I'm saying that filth showed no interest at all in them... And so, Araragi."

Then—utterly free of abashment or affectation, Senjogahara spoke the words.

"I'm kissing you."

"........."

Scary.

You're being scary, Miss Hitagi.

"No, that's not it," she told herself. "Could I... bother you... for a kiss? What would... think to... about... a kiss..."

"..............."

"Let's kiss, Araragi."

"So that's what you're going to settle on."

It wasn't too inappropriate a way to phrase it.

In fact, no way to phrase it could be more her.

And so—today became a memorable day.

For us.

004

Now on to Wednesday, June fourteenth, or the day after I woke from my dreams—and by that, I of course mean that our romantic astronomical observations ended without incident, Daddy Senjogahara drove us another two hours back to the town where we lived, I got to bed at around one a.m., had some trivial dream of the kind you mostly forget, woke from that dream, and got out of bed—rather than that my first date with Senjogahara the previous night was all a dream. I was pedaling my way to school, sleepily, when I found Hachikuji.

Mayoi Hachikuji.

Pigtails, her bangs so short her eyebrows showed.

A girl in fifth grade who wore a backpack.

"Whoa there."

I stopped pedaling.

She hadn't noticed me yet. Glancing from side to side, she seemed to be enjoying a morning walk.

Hmm. It felt like it had been a while since we last met.

Well, it had been about two weeks since I saw her. It wasn't what you could objectively call "a while" when I thought about it, but for some reason I felt overjoyed to have run into Hachikuji. It's even harder to get in touch with a fifth grader than a girl in junior high, after all.

I had some spare time, unlike before. It couldn't hurt to have a bit of a discussion with her (I took the liberty of assuming that Hachikuji was free). The question then was how to get her attention... I began by getting off my bike, careful not to make a sound. I put down my kickstand and parked my bike on the side of the road.

All right, now.

Then again, this was Hachikuji I was dealing with.

Under no circumstances did I want her to realize that I was happy. There was the chance she would start getting carried away if I showed her any such hints. I couldn't aggravate her cheekiness. What did I need? An unconcerned, no, an uncaring "Oh, huh. You're here? I just so happened to say hi to you because I didn't have anything better to be doing," with a little tap on the shoulder? Right, I wasn't so frivolous that I'd burst into cheer over seeing a friend again. At my age, I wanted to sell myself as someone dry and cool.

Okay.

So sneak up to her from behind, then...

"HA-chikujiii! It's been ages, you little scamp!"

I snuck up to her from behind, then latched onto her with a hug.

"Eeeek?!" the girl shrieked.

Undeterred, I embraced her with all my strength as if to crush her small body, then rubbed my cheeks against hers over and over again.

"Hahahaha! Oh, you're just so cute! Lemme touch you more, lemme hug you more! I'm gonna get a peek at those panties, you lovable little lady!"

"Eeek! Eeek! Eeep!" Hachikuji continued to loudly shriek, until it turned into a "Grrah!"

Now she was biting me.

"Grrah, grrah, grrah!"

"That hurts! What're you doing?!"

The words really should have been directed at myself.

Both the "hurts" and the "what're you doing."

"Ssshh! Fssshh!"

I was brought back to my senses at last after being bitten in at least three discrete spots, but now Hachikuji's hair was standing on end like a Super Saiyan's as she emitted the kinds of threatening noises you'd expect from a wildcat.

Well, of course she would.

"I-It's okay, it's okay. I'm not an enemy."

"Ssshh! Ssshh!"

"C'mon, calm down. Deep breaths."

"Fssshh... Kuhhh-huhhh... Kuhhh-huhhh..."

"......"

Now her breathing sounded like some sort of mechanized villain's.

Actually, Hachikuji hadn't spoken a single word resembling human language since she first appeared in this scene.

"Hey, look, it's me. The friendly guy that everyone in the neighborhood knows... The guy who once showed you the way when you were a lost little lamb..."

"Mm... Ah..."

Hachikuji's eyes seemed to recognize me at last. Her bristling hair slowly returned to normal.

"Oh, if it isn't Mister Ararandy."

"Don't call me names that make me sound sexually frustrated. It's Araragi."

"I'm sorry. Slip of the tongue."

She might have been technically right for once, having been biting me... At least this time around, maybe I was to blame for the nickname as well as for getting bitten.

I hadn't been able to control my emotions.

I'd gone out of control.

I might've still been feeling high from what had happened the day before, too.

"Oh? So I see you're wearing your summer uniform, Mister Araragi," Hachikuji said. She seemed fine now. Maybe she was just stupid. "Hmm, you're slim despite your muscular build, which means that short sleeves don't look any good on you at all."

"What am I supposed to do in the summer, in that case?"

Sleeveless shirts and the like weren't in fashion for boys. It's not as if they're remotely cute or anything when guys wear them, either.

"It could be that the problem isn't short-sleeve shirts," she answered, "but that dress shirts don't look good on you. Oh, and you looked so wonderful in that high-collared jacket. What would you say to wearing that year-round?"

"I'm not in the male cheerleading squad…"

Incidentally, Naoetsu High didn't have one.

We weren't that into clubs and sports.

"And while your sleeves have gotten shorter," observed Hachikuji, "your hair has gotten longer. Your face is every bit as docile as your personality is savage, so you're going to end up looking like a girl if you grow it out any more."

"I have to grow it out like this. I'll admit that it'll feel like too much over the summer, though. Also, I don't want to hear you calling me savage."

"Isn't having a girly name enough for you?"

"You're really milking that one. What about your hair? Those twin tails look like a monster straight out of *Ultraman*."

"That's just the name, not the appearance."

"Okay, true."

"Your hair looks like it belongs to an alien from Planet Afro."

"Hold on! I'm pretty sure Planet Afro is something you just made up, but whatever aliens come from there, they're obviously going to have afros! I'm growing my hair out long and straight!"

"You say that, but your presence is so thin that you'd be a character without sprite art in a dating sim. Whoever claims it first wins. If I say they have afros, they have afros. If I say they have dreads, they have dreads."

"Really?! O-Okay, Hachikuji, quick! Say I'm a tall, broad-shouldered, macho dude!"

"The very fact you listed those qualities proves you're none of them… But is that your ideal image of yourself? A tall, broad-shouldered, and macho dude?"

"Hey, why do you look so unamused?"

"Oh. You seem to be bleeding from your head, Mister Araragi."

"Some savage person bit me."

"Quick, you ought to tie off your neck and stop the bleeding."

"That'd kill me!"

How could I explain it?

I loved Senjogahara best and got along with Kanbaru better than anyone else, but for whatever reason, I had the most fun talking to Hachikuji.

Was it that my heart was being soothed by a grade schooler?

"It's fine," I said. "Something like this will heal in no time."

"Oh, that was right. You're a vampire, aren't you, Mister Araragi."

"Well, a mockery of one."

Over spring break—I was attacked by a vampire.

Just as a cat bewitched Hanekawa, a crab met Senjogahara, a snail led Hachikuji astray, a monkey heard Kanbaru's wish, and a snake trapped Sengoku—a demon attacked me.

I grew my hair out to hide the wounds from that day.

It wasn't a vampire hunter, Christian special forces, or a kin-slaying vampire, but a frivolous dude in a Hawaiian shirt who was passing by, Mèmè Oshino, who plucked me from my predicament for the time being—but not without aftereffects.

My body was extraordinarily good at healing itself.

"Healing…" said Hachikuji. "In that case, there's something I'd like to try."

"Something you'd like to try?"

"Indeed. If we split you in half down the median line with a chainsaw or something, would we get two Mister Araragis?"

"That's some messed-up stuff, grade schooler!"

I'm not an earthworm!

Why would she ever think that'd work?!

"I'm joking," she assured. "I would never do something like that to you, not after all you've done for me."

"Oh… Yeah, I guess not. We're friends, after all."

"Yes. Tearing you limb from limb still wouldn't be enough, so how could I possibly settle for cutting you in half?"

"………"

Maybe she wasn't fine after all.

I'd incurred a grudge.

"Just you wait, Mister Araragi. I'm going to open up a ladder when you least expect it and watch as you walk right under."

"Wh-What?! How many years would that take off my life expectancy?!"

"And that's not all. I'm going to be the one sneaking up behind you next time. I'll slowly run my finger down along your spine."

"Y-You monster! You're going to make me beg you to run it slowly back up?!"

"Oh, I'm only getting started. This is what happens when you make me mad, you poor thing. I have a feeling you're going to learn what true fear is."

"Heh," I snorted at that point. "You'd better watch what you say, Hachikuji."

"Excuse me?"

"You're going to be the one learning about true fear. Just try and get me to walk under a ladder…because I'll respond with violence!"

There he was, a high schooler threatening a kid with violence over fears that he might lose a few years from walking under a ladder.

Yes, me.

"It's not too late to apologize," I said. "I'll still forgive you."

"Ha…"

But this was why she's my eternal rival.

Hachikuji was now the one laughing fearlessly.

"Mister Araragi, you'd better dutch what you say."

"Dutch?! Am I going to have to apologize to the Netherlands now?! What did I ever do to them?!"

"If you don't hurry up and say sorry, you'll find yourself on the receiving end of the Whirling Dance of Windmills."

"What is that, some kind of super move?!"

"Apologize now, unless you want to meet Don Quixote's fate."

"That was in Spain, though!"

"So, what now? Are you so eager to earn the name of Don?"

How had we gotten here?

But I certainly didn't want to be called Don.

"Mister Araragi, I can't believe you haven't apologized yet… Either you're thick-headed, you're thick-headed, you're thick-headed, or I ought to rephrase myself."

"So we're talking a three-quarters likelihood that I'm thick-headed... Jeez... Yeah, yeah, I get it. I need to apologize to the Dutch."

"When you say yes, one hundred times should be enough."

"I don't even want to try!"

"It's your only chance to yescape."

"Aren't you the little comedian!"

Hold on.

Did she not want an apology for herself?

"I'm not as generous as the Dutch," she said. "You're sorely mistaken if you think an apology is all you need to earn my forgiveness."

"You think highly of the Dutch, don't you..."

"If you really seek my forgiveness...I'll accept a year's worth of sponge cake."

"Well, if that's all you're going to demand..."

"A year's worth means three a day, though."

"That's a lot of money!"

It easily came out to over a hundred thousand yen.

She was fleecing me.

"Well," I said anyway, "I am grateful for your forgiveness."

"Oh, no. No thanks."

"......"

Could she have thought that "No thanks" means "No need to thank me"?

Wow.

"Mister Araragi, you must be on your way to school. What a hard worker you are. I forget, did you say that your attendance record was a concern?"

"Yeah. I might even have to repeat a year thanks to the hole I got myself in during my first two years. But this is no time for me to be worried about something as basic as that. Now I have my sights set a tier higher."

"A tier higher, you say? What an odd choice of words. What could you mean by that?"

"Up until now, my goal was to graduate, but—"

Er, wait. Was it okay to tell her?

Then again, I wouldn't have to worry about her telling anyone else. In fact, maybe I should have been telling as many people as I could just to put more pressure on myself.

"I'm going to be focusing on exams now."

"Exams? Oh, elementary exit exams?"

"I'm almost out of high school, why would I be taking those now?!"

I explained my circumstances just as I had to Hanekawa and Kanbaru. Hachikuji, an excellent listener despite what you may be led to believe, kept me talking as she nodded and said, "Is that so," "I see," "Which means," "I should have expected as much," "I never knew," and so on at the right moments. Of course, the words coming easily to me must have also had something to do with the fact that this was my third time saying them.

......

But becoming adept at describing your goals meant that you hadn't accomplished them... What good was it going to do me if I was all bark?

Goals need to become results.

"Mister Araragi, it sounds like much has happened since we last met. It was a wise person who said to pay close attention to any young man you haven't seen for three days."

"Heh... What can I say?"

"It feels like it went by in a flash," Hachikuji said, her voice somber.

Somber, yet somehow nostalgic.

"So it's been three years since that day..."

"No! It hasn't been that long!"

Two weeks!

Don't make it sound like the series finale!

"Was it, now? Well, I suppose if it only took you two weeks to come to that decision, you're just as likely to reverse it in the next couple of weeks. I mustn't be so quick to take you at your word. A change that takes place over three days takes only three more days to undo. If you don't see a young man for six days, he's back where he began."

"You say some mean things, you know."

But she was right.

In fact, I hadn't perused a page of those study aids Hanekawa picked out for me the day before yesterday.

"Aah," said Hachikuji, "so you're one of those people who feels satisfied just buying a study aid. Yes, I know the type. I myself often buy video games but never play them, satisfied with the purchase alone."

"I'm worried if you're already doing that as a grade schooler..."

And it wasn't as if my determination had wavered and I hadn't gone through those study aids because it was too much effort... It just so happened that I spotted Sengoku at the exact same bookstore where I bought them, which got me wrapped up dealing with an aberration, sleeping in an abandoned cram school like a canned sardine, going back home to get some more sleep, heading to school only to have to work on the culture festival—and going on a date with Senjogahara.

When could I have flipped through my study aids?

"A date? Doesn't that count as playing?"

"Urk..."

She was right.

Honestly, Hachikuji said, appalled. "'Busy' is just an excuse that people who can't budget their time like to use. If you wanted, you could have checked out those study aids during your breaks at school, for example. You're being bound by a preconceived notion, a prejudice, that studying is something you only do during classes or at home."

"Whoa... That's actually solid advice."

Yeah.

She was right again.

"Hachikuji, all this time I might've wrongly thought of you as a hopelessly dumb kid. Are you actually a fairly passable student? You told me before that your grades weren't very good, but were you just being modest to avoid hurting my feelings?"

"Who knows? I've never studied in my life before."

"........."

She was a fool.

Or wait, maybe an incredible natural?

Which was she... I needed to test her.

"Hachikuji, let's play a little word game. I'll say a word, then you say a word that starts with the last letter of my word, and then I'll do the same for your word. The first person who ends a word with the letter E loses. Okay? Let's start with…News!"

"Slug!"

"Gorilla!"

"Apple!"

"What? I've never seen anyone lose that fast before!"

What an imbecile.

Actually, she was playing along.

Instead of immediately losing with something like "Snake," she waited a beat, subtly showing taste. She wasn't just fun to talk to, she was so talented that I needed to bring her home and make a habit of chatting with her for thirty minutes every night before I went to sleep.

Still, she sounded like an imbecile even if I couldn't discount the possibility that she was a natural who could play along. I hadn't come close to accomplishing my initial goal.

I needed to try again.

Time for another test.

"I'm going to ask you a riddle next, Hachikuji."

"I'll accept the challenge, naturally. I've never turned my back to an enemy. You aren't one, but if you're coming at me, I won't hold back. You'll learn to fear me."

"I have two heads and three eyes. I have four mouths and a hundred teeth. I have seven arms and five legs, and I'm small but can swallow an elephant whole. What animal am I?"

"…One of your friends?"

"A loon! Because I'd have to be one to think something like that could exist! So no, I don't have any friend who fits the description! Would you want that as a friend of a friend?!"

I'm selective about my friends!

Urk… If I considered her answer a clever way to turn the tables on me, I still couldn't gauge her intellect… As I thought this, Hachikuji opened her mouth.

"Let me ask you one in return. I have the head of a monkey, the body of a tanuki, the limbs of a tiger, the tail of a snake, and the cry of a thrush. What animal am I?"

"A loon, because you'd have to be one to think something like that exists?"

"A Nue."

"........."

She was right.

I felt like I'd been dealt a loss.

Could this elementary schoolgirl be a natural after all?

Damn. There was too much to her for me to see all of her at once.

"I'm surprised a grade school kid like you knows what a Nue is, though."

"I study many subjects."

"Is that so."

"Anyway, Mister Weraragi."

"Don't call me names that make it sound like I've transformed. It's Araragi."

"Excuse me. Slip of the tongue."

"No, you did it on purpose…"

"Shlip of the tongue."

"Or maybe not?!"

"Snip off the tongue."

"Too pious!"

Now that it was the seventh time we were going through this established routine, I was starting to get the hang of it.

It had gone off flawlessly.

"Anyway, Mister Araragi. You ought to know that studying for exams is no easy task."

"Yeah, I know that by now."

"Oh, do you. I don't, myself."

"I had my doubts!"

She hadn't ever sat for such exams.

"Even so," she said, "I'm really worried about you. I don't want to sound like an old wife, but will you be able to fill out that college application?"

"That's what you're worried about?! Beware the little old wife!"

"If you do complete the application, the rest is staying in good health for the big day. You'll be able to take your exams."

"No! I'm trying to do more than just take them, I need to pass them too!"

"So you're studying for them… Well, I may have been uncharacteristically negative, but I'm sure you'll be fine. You're the kind of person who can do it if he tries."

"Oh. You really think so?"

"Of course. Now that you've decided to take those exams, you're as good as accepted."

"Wow, you'd go that far?"

"I haven't gone far enough. You aren't just as good as accepted, it may not be an exaggeration to say you've graduated."

"Hold on, Hachikuji, that's definitely overstating things. All I've done is decide to take some exams."

"No, I can already see you with your doctorate in hand. That's right, from this day onward, I'll be calling you Doctor."

"It's fine, call me whatever you want. So that's how you see me? Can't criticize you there."

"Then allow me to call you by the Latin, to make you sound all the more academic."

"What's a doctorate called in Latin?"

"Pedophiae Doltoris."

"Shut up! And that setup took forever!"

Even I was getting tired waiting for the punch line!

I was starting to think there might not be one!

"A pedo and a dolt, Pedophiae Doltoris… It's as if the term was made for you."

"No term ever gets made for me, okay?! I'll admit I'm a dolt, but I'm no pedo! I lead an upstanding life!"

"And if you squint your eyes, you may start seeing 'dope' in the first word, too."

"Stop! Stop it right now before you ruin the word 'doctorate' for me forever!"

"Just don't get drunk on sweet platitudes like 'You can do it if you try.' The only people who say that are those who don't try."

Hachikuji sounded all serious now.

Big words coming from someone who'd never studied before…

"Gosh," I objected, "you think you can get away with saying anything. What a fresh brat, I'm starting to want to punish you."

"'What a fresh boob, I'm starting to want to punish you?' You sometimes say the lewdest things."

"That's not what I said!"

"I'm shocked you came up with a line that sounds so lewd if we just replaced 'brat' with 'boob.'"

"What line wouldn't sound lewd if you replaced a key word with 'boob'?!"

What a conversation. We were saying things based on momentum alone.

"But yes, you're right," I admitted. "I'm going to need to hang in there."

"Yes. Go hang yourself in your room."

"I'm not gonna! But you know, thanks to my excellent tutors, I think I'm good. They'd never allow me to slack off. I'm going to be studying day in and day out, whether I want to or not. Heh, actually, I'm unstoppable with the best and seventh-best students in my year on my side."

"Good, how forward of you."

"………"

She thought that meant "positive" or "optimistic," didn't she…

"But Mister Araragi, will things really go so smoothly? Those two ladies, however renowned, are taking on the absolute worst student in their year…"

"I've never scored last, thank you! I actually did pretty well this time around! You need to listen to what I say!"

"To your boasts? I don't think so. You're only interesting when you air your misfortunes. Explore that subject a little further, will you?"

"Why should I bully myself like that?!"

"Then allow Mayoi Hachikuji, as unqualified as she is, to speak on your behalf. It's time for Mister Araragi's Proud Tales of Misfortune.

'Everything came up smelling like roses, but Mister Araragi was allergic to them!'"

"Stop making up sad stories about me! I like roses! They smell great! And I'm fine with pollens, as far as I know!"

"His selling point is that when things seem to be going well for him, they're actually not when he stops to think about it."

"That's not me! Stop giving me weird character traits that will make me think twice whatever I do!"

"Mister Araragi's Proud Tales of Misfortune, part two."

"You even have a part two?! Did the first one become a top-grossing Hollywood hit or something?!"

"'Mister Araragi felt his tummy grumbling in the middle of the night, so he decided to make some instant noodles. But despite being billed as instant, they were surprisingly hard to make!'"

"D-Damn! I want to shoot you down, but that's actually happened to me more than once! A rare example of the sequel being the real masterpiece!"

"It's Friday the thirteenth for Koyomi Araragi, now and forever."

"That really makes me want to give up!"

"Still, the best and the seventh-best in your year, huh," Hachikuji brought us back on track there. "Miss Hanekawa…I met the other day. The lady with the braids, correct?"

"Yeah… Now that you mention it, I guess you know both of them."

"And Miss Senjogahara—is your girlfriend."

"Yep."

"Hmm." Hachikuji folded her arms with a troubled expression. She seemed to be thinking about something, a look that didn't suit her.

"What, got something to say about that?"

"No, simply that the normal choice between the two would be Miss Hanekawa. It struck me as odd that you chose Miss Senjogahara instead."

"Odd…"

How was I supposed to answer that one?

Why was she wondering?

"I think both of them are pretty," she continued, "but their personalities are like day and night. Miss Hanekawa is like a kind older sister—while Miss Senjogahara is, well…malice personified."

"Well, I don't think Senjogahara would want to hear that coming from you."

Then again, Senjogahara had said some awful things to Hachikuji, so it made sense. In comparison, Hanekawa had been kind to Hachikuji.

She was kind—and stern.

Just like an older sister should be.

The choice might have seemed odd to a child.

"You see," I explained, "I don't see Hanekawa in that way—she's someone I'm indebted to. I can't go into details, though. Hanekawa would probably turn me down, anyway. And Senjogahara's personality is part of the reason why I…"

Uhm.

Yeah, it was hard to finish that sentence.

I trailed off and left it at that.

"I see." Instead of being mean and hounding me, Hachikuji nodded. "How ironic."

"What do you mean?"

"You don't understand? Then let me put it another way. How ionic."

"That makes even less sense to me??"

"Well, you're the type to pursue Lindt in *Quiz Nanairo Dreams*. You must have odd taste in the opposite sex."

"Don't you think that reference needs to be explained?!"

This one was really obscure.

Okay, a while back there was this dating-sim quiz arcade game that CAPCOM developed called *Quiz Nanairo Dreams: The Miracle of Rainbow Village*, where you answered trivia questions and got to become friends with seven featured female characters. You raise their impression of you over half a year before finally defeating the resurrected Demon King at the end to live happily ever after with your favorite girl; only, along the way, there is this character named Lindt, one of the Demon King's flunkies who gets in your way, and though she happens to be a girl, you sadly can't end up with her no matter what tricks and techniques you may try. There's no telling how many hundred-yen coins disappeared into those machines in search of a happy end with her. As a note, there was a proper route for Lindt in the home release of the game, perhaps due to player demand. Okay, commentary over!

"Very impressive of you to know, Mister Araragi."

"Oh, it's nothing… Hey, don't bring up references that require this much explanation in the first place! Even *Bikkuriman* was better! I think I'm the first person to go on about *Quiz Nanairo Dreams* since we entered the twenty-first century!"

"But if we continue to wage a low-key grassroots campaign, they might create a remake some day."

"Too low-key!"

"But if you say you prefer Miss Senjogahara, that must be how it is. To each his scorn."

"'To each his own,' yes?!"

"Incidentally," Hachikuji said, suddenly changing the subject. Why was she pouring cold water on the subject right as we were getting warmed up? It was unlike her. "You told me the other day about a vampire—a vampiress who went and turned you into a mockery of a human of a mockery of a vampire. Oh, what was she called now. Miss Shinobu Oshino?"

"Huh? Oh."

I did tell her.

I guess on Mother's Day, when we first met?

Hachikuji continued, "A child of about eight, with blond hair, and a helmet with goggles on top…I believe you said?"

"Yeah. What about her?"

"I've never been introduced to her so I have no way of saying for sure, but I spotted your Miss Shinobu yesterday."

"What?"

Shinobu?

Hachikuji—had seen her?

"Was this shabby older dude near her?" I asked. "Visibly frivolous, and in a tacky, psychedelic Hawaiian shirt that no self-respecting person would wear nowadays?"

"Hmm? I'm having difficulty understanding you, but are you trying to ask me if you were by the girl's side?"

"No! Do you see me as a shabby older dude?! And never in my life have I worn a Hawaiian shirt, not even with the most boring design imaginable!"

"You shouldn't say things about others that you wouldn't want said about yourself."

"You're absolutely right!"

The truth hurts.

It always does.

"In any case, Mister Araragi, this blond child was alone. No one was near her."

"Hmm... Around what time was this?"

"I believe it was about five in the afternoon."

"Five..."

I would have still had my hands full preparing for the culture festival.

Before I talked to Sengoku by the gates.

"Where was this?"

"Near the donut shop along the highway."

"Oh, there... You take some long walks, don't you? That's a pretty big habitat for a kid... But okay, a donut shop."

It was a Mister Donut.

The detail made the story seem a bit more believable.

But Shinobu—alone?

Could that really have happened?

Of course, we were in a boring town in the middle of nowhere, Japan... You rarely saw anyone with their hair dyed brown, so a blond? Who else could it be but Shinobu? If you added the helmet and goggles on top of that... But could Shinobu travel that far from the abandoned cram school? I'd convinced myself for no real reason that Shinobu couldn't leave, but...now that I thought about it, Oshino had never said anything like that. Would he really allow her to act on her own, though?

"Yes. I thought the same thing," Hachikuji said. "If she really is a vampire then I'm no match for her, so I dared not get a step closer. But

I did think it would be best to inform you, which is why I was waiting here today to ambush you."

"Oh, really?"

So this wasn't a chance meeting. Now that she mentioned it, she did seem to be looking around when I first saw her.

Another day where someone was waiting on me.

"You should have told me that first, then," I scolded.

"I'm sorry. I'd forgotten from the shock of being grabbed from behind by some pedophile who then rubbed his cheek against mine."

"A pedophile? Do we really have any of those in this town? As an upstanding local, I can't abide that."

"It's okay. Let's have a big heart for these small people. The slogan of the month in my class is 'Be kind to pedophiles.'"

"What kind of school are you attending?! Are you sure you're okay there?!"

In short, it was my own fault.

I was reaping what I'd sown.

"Huh, okay then," I said. "Sorry to get you so worked up over this. Thanks, I think I'll go straight to Oshino's place and see what's going on, maybe even today."

"Oh no, I'm just glad I could be of service to you, Mister Araragi."

If anything, shouldn't you be worried about the time, asked Hachikuji. I looked at the watch around my right wrist. Hmm, we'd been talking for a while. Time really does fly when you're having fun…

When would I get to meet Hachikuji next?

Oh well.

"Do you have a cell phone?" I absurdly tried asking a grade schooler. This was the kind of town where even middle schoolers didn't have them.

"Hmm. I'm sad to say that I'm exceedingly bad with mechanical devices."

"Is that so."

"Yes. I might not be able to watch television after 2010."

"Even digital broadcasting is too much for you…"

It went beyond being good or bad with tech.

Even Kanbaru and Oshino weren't that incapable.

"What could they mean by '1seg'?" she wondered out loud.

"You sound so stupid…"

Hmm.

Well, there was nothing I could do.

I'd have to leave this one to fate.

Maybe running into her now and then while I wandered around town was the right relationship to have with Hachikuji. I shouldn't be too greedy, and coincidences were precious in their own way. If she needed to see me, like today, she seemed to have no problem doing so.

I got back on my bike.

"Okay, Hachikuji. See you later."

"All right. I know we'll meet again."

My fifth-grade friend saw me off as I headed to school. With barely any time left to spare, I was pedaling hard.

Mayoi Hachikuji. In any case, I was glad she was doing fine—but her situation was too precarious for me to be putting it that way. You could say she was in the worst position out of everyone I knew that had met an aberration.

That said—it wasn't as though I could do anything.

I shouldn't be thinking that I could.

People—just went and got saved on their own.

I shouldn't get that mixed up.

I knew I couldn't, and yet.

"………"

Three months had passed since I first met an aberration—since I first learned of aberrations.

Three years it was not. But.

I had still gone through a lot of changes in that time.

Did I then—

Just go and change on my own?

I managed to walk through the school gates before the warning bell rang. Actually, the volleyball shorts and school swimsuit I'd received from Sengoku to give back to Kanbaru were in my bag. My plan had been to get to school early and visit her second-year classroom, but now... Hmm, I didn't have enough time. It was fine, though. I couldn't give it to her in plain sight anyway, and considering the hassle of summoning her from her classroom, during lunch break or after school made more sense. As I figured this out, I parked my bicycle in my spot on the school's lot.

I walked into the building and began climbing the stairs.

Then my cell phone began to vibrate.

Oops, I needed to turn it off before heading into class... That was careless. The vibration ended immediately, so could it be a text instead of a phone call? This early, though? Maybe it was my little sisters... Senjogahara and Kanbaru weren't people who went out of their way to use text messages. I took my phone out of my pocket and checked the screen. I doubted my own eyes when I saw the sender, but those doubts were wiped away when I read the body of the message. In all of Japan and its long history, only one person would begin a mere text message with "Salutations" and end with "Sincerely yours in haste."

Reading what was between that "Salutations" and "Sincerely yours in haste"—and rereading it, I stopped in my tracks on the stairs to class and immediately headed straight back the way I came.

Against the flow of students.

Straight back to the bike parking lot.

"Oh."

There I ran into Hitagi Senjogahara. The warning bell was moments away—but unlike me, she hadn't been moments away from being late. As if she calculated everything so as not to waste a single moment, Senjogahara always came to school just in time.

Seeing her so suddenly after what had happened yesterday, I felt a little embarrassed and was at a brief loss for words. But Hitagi Senjogahara had the same flat-as-can-be attitude and expression as ever.

"What, Araragi," she said, "are you going somewhere?"

"Just around the corner."

"What for?"

"Call it humanitarian aid."

"Is that so."

She was indifferent.

Yes, that was Hitagi Senjogahara.

She had me figured out.

Another case of wordless communication—or so I hoped.

"Fine. Then be on your way, Araragi. I'd normally never even consider it, but taking pity on you this one time, I'll answer for you during roll call."

"We only have forty kids in our class, I don't think that would work... In fact, I'm afraid you'll only get the teacher mad at you."

"Don't worry, I can do this. I'll be sure to imitate your voice. I have an excellent VA playing my role."

"Voice actress?! Is this world an anime?!"

"'I'm not going to let Kanbaru meet an unfortunate fate at anyone's hands! Even if those hands are yours!' What do you think, did that sound like you?"

"Not even close! You got my hopes up, but it sounded even less like me than I thought possible! And don't pick out such an embarrassing line to repeat! I sense malice in your choice!"

"Kanbaru cried tears of joy when I told her about that one."

"Don't go around making our juniors cry over something so inane! You're not her only trusted senior now, you realize!"

"'Miss Hitagi...you're so beautiful. I couldn't ask for anyone better than you. I love you.' What do you think, did that sound like you?"

"Not even close, and I haven't spoken that line yet!"

"Yet? You mean you plan to?"

"..., ...kk, yes!"

That's how it went.

I had nothing resembling the time to be having such a stupid conversation, but I still thanked Senjogahara for calming my rattled nerves before running on to the bike lot even faster than before.

005

That park—I still didn't know if its name was read "Rohaku" or "Nami-shiro" or something else entirely. And if I still didn't know, I doubted I ever would—but speaking of memorable, perhaps the park was a place to remember.

Because of that one Mother's Day—when I arrived at this park that lacked any playground equipment other than a swing, after wandering around on my beloved mountain bike (back when it still took that shape), and ran into Senjogahara who was out on a walk and encountered a lost Mayoi Hachikuji.

And I still remembered.

That day—not only did I happen to meet those two, but I also saw Tsubasa Hanekawa. Yes, she'd told me something then—that she lived in the area.

The fact that her text asked me to meet at the very same park was neither a coincidence nor, I thought, some allusion. In her wisdom, Hanekawa simply chose the one landmark near her home that I knew, this park with the indecipherable name. Her deft hand when it came to these matters always had my vote.

Yes—

Tsubasa Hanekawa had sent me that message.

Forget about the warning bell, the late bell had gone off long ago. Not only that, it took a bit of time to arrive at the park. It was in an unfamiliar area, and I'd only been to it once after going wherever the streets took me. Despite it all, around the end of the first period I managed to appear in front of Hanekawa, who was sitting on a bench with her back rounded, shrinking.

Her appearance gave off a very different impression than usual.

It was extreme even for a makeover.

Her light long-sleeved blouse almost seemed to conceal her upper body and had noticeably long arms. The pants that protruded from below it were also baggy. They were pink, a gaudy color to wear for just stepping outside—and instead of the school-specified plain white socks and shoes that she customarily stuck to, she had opted for the more carefree bare feet and sandals.

Her glasses were the same as ever, but her braids had come undone. No, that wasn't entirely correct. Not even a class president among class presidents, elected not by her classmates but the gods themselves, was born with her hair braided. Especially this early in the morning—the right way to put it was that she had yet to tie her hair in braids. It was the first time I'd seen Hanekawa with her hair untied... Naturally enough, it seemed fairly long now that it wasn't. Longer than Senjogahara's, from the looks of it.

Hanekawa was wearing a hunting cap on top of that hair.

A hat was another first.

"...Oh, Araragi."

Hanekawa finally noticed me. Cradling herself and looking down at the ground, she must not have, even though I was standing right in front of her.

Her expression was a touch uneasy.

Or so it seemed to me.

"Tut-tut," she cautioned me first thing. "You shouldn't ride your bike all the way into the park. They have bike parking, so you need to use it."

That's Hanekawa for you.

"Now's not the time," I reminded her. "Are you going to chide me about my bicycle of all things after making me skip school?"

"This and that are separate issues. Now hurry up and park it."

" ...... "

Hmph. She really wasn't having any of it.

Was she not going to start with some words of gratitude for me? I had run over to her like a faithful little dog.

But nothing was going to come of complaining here.

Hanekawa was right, too.

Saying "Fine," I got off my bike and pushed it to the distant parking area. The same rusted and broken-down bicycles from May fourteenth were still parked there, unchanged. I put my bike next to them and locked it. Since there were still no signs of any man, woman, or child in the park (this seemed to be a constant, whether it was a weekday or a holiday), I didn't see much point in locking up my bike...

I returned to the park.

Hanekawa was sitting on the bench.

The light blouse was hiding some of her baggy pants, but I was certain they were pajamas, given their color and material... So that meant she was wearing pajamas on the top, too? And her sandals looked like slip-ons. Had she woken up, gotten straight out of bed, put on nothing more than a blouse, and left home?

"I'm sorry, Araragi," she apologized to me when I returned.

Though they weren't words of gratitude.

"I made you skip school."

"Oh, never mind," I said. "Did it come across that way to you? I wasn't trying to be sarcastic."

"Don't worry, though—I calculated it all out. You won't have any problems at all given today's schedule, even if you skip the whole day."

" ...... "

Those were nasty calculations.

To be doing that even when she asked for help...

She really did think too hard about everything. Didn't that mean she wouldn't have sent me the text if the day's scheduling were a problem for my attendance or could cause some other issue?

She thought too much about consequences.

I tried asking, "With the class president and vice president missing, what's going to happen to the culture festival prep? Do you have some kind of plan for that, too?"

"I called the teacher's lounge after sending you that text... I told Hoshina about the work that needs to be done today and how to do it."

"..."

God, she had her act together.

How about the way she called our teacher after texting me so she could make good use of her time waiting at the park?

"Senjogahara is going to be in charge after school," Hanekawa informed me.

"What? Are you sure you're not making a mistake?"

My girlfriend hated nothing more than working with, and for, others. I could imagine no greater hybrid of the two than preparing for a culture festival. No "Caution: Do Not Mix" warning could be big enough.

"Senjogahara skipped yesterday. This is to make up for that."

"Hunh..."

Against Hanekawa, all of Senjogahara's audacity and defiance amounted to nothing... Well, our class still saw her as the cloistered princess, so if asked, she would at least carry out her duties no doubt...

"I'm glad you're a good person," I said. "There's no one more calculating than you, so just imagine what would happen if you used that brain of yours for evil."

"That's not true. As far as how calculating I am...it was pretty risky of me to bet on your cell phone being on. I couldn't try calling you first, either, because you might already be on the premises at that hour..."

"Huh? Couldn't you call and hang up after one ring if you wanted to see if my phone was on?"

"If I did, you'd try to call me back, being the principled person you are. Right?"

"Oh, so you'd even seen through my personality."

So receiving a text was fine, but calling back wasn't... That was pretty subtle. It seemed like a tough choice for Hanekawa, too. I'd thought I didn't have the time, but now I was glad I'd texted her back at a stop light on my way to the park.

My chat with Hachikuji had been meaningful, then—if I'd arrived at school earlier, I'd have turned my phone off in our classroom.

......

Well, putting that aside.

Knowing that someone was in her pajamas flustered me even if that someone was Hanekawa... It was my first time witnessing something as extraordinary as a girl in her nightwear (cases involving my two little sisters don't count).

Her blouse was the one lamentable part. I could make out only the pants, and just from the legs down, which lacked that finishing touch... or should I say, it had the final touch and nothing else? People talk about tantalizing glimpses, but this felt like starving.

Wasn't there some way to get that bland thing off of her?

You know, like in "The North Wind and the Sun."

"Hey, Hanekawa."

"What?"

"Er—Miss Hanekawa."

"Miss?"

"Allow me to take your blouse for you."

"......"

Ack.

She couldn't have looked any more unamused.

I had tried my best to imitate a waiter at a fancy restaurant greeting a valued customer, but that charade wasn't going to be persuasive in an open-air park.

"Araragi."

"Yes?"

"You're going to make me mad."

"...I'm sorry."

It was a beam of blinding sobriety.

I felt like getting on all fours and begging for her forgiveness.

"All right," I said, "enough joking around—what happened, Hanekawa? You didn't tell me what the actual problem was in your message, but...is it those headaches?"

"Yeah—the headaches..." Hanekawa said slowly, "are gone now."

"Oh? They are?"

"I guess you could say they've ended…"

Hanekawa was choosing her words carefully.

Choosing—or rather, she couldn't express herself without coining new ones, such seemed to be her situation.

I had an idea what it was, to be honest.

I did.

"Um—Araragi? About Golden Week. I…remembered."

"Oh—you did."

Her headache.

That—was the significance of her headaches.

"Well, maybe not," she continued. "It's more like I remembered that I'm forgetting something…but no matter how hard I try, I can only recall a hazy image."

"Oh—yeah, I'd imagine as much. It shouldn't be possible for you to remember it all to the end."

Actually, remembering that she'd ever forgotten should have been impossible for her in the first place. Hanekawa was never supposed to recall those nine nightmarish days—

And yet.

"Until now…I'd vaguely known that you and Mister Oshino saved me, but…it's so strange. Not only could I not remember how, but from what—it's like I was under some weird hypnosis."

"Hypnosis, huh…"

Well, it was something else entirely.

But I could see where she was coming from.

She said, "I still don't feel a hundred percent about this—but I'm glad I remembered. At last, I can give you and Mister Oshino my proper thanks."

"Oh—but we didn't save you. As Oshino says—"

"I just went and got saved on my own—right?"

"Right."

Absolutely right.

Especially when it came to me. I hadn't done a thing.

When it came to the case of Hanekawa's cat, Shinobu had done the most. If there was anyone whom Hanekawa needed to thank, it wasn't me or Mèmè Oshino, but Shinobu Oshino, the little blonde.

"A cat," Hanekawa said. "A cat—right?"

"…"

"I recalled that part—the cat from *back then*, right? *The one you and I buried together—that cat.* Yeah…I recalled that part."

"Well—*you were still you* back then."

"Huh?"

"Er, nothing—but Hanekawa. You didn't summon me here *just because you remembered*—did you?"

No matter how much my attendance record wasn't going to be an issue, she wasn't going to make me play hooky over something like that.

Not only had she remembered, *there was something after that*—the recollection had to be secondary.

"That's right," Hanekawa affirmed.

She was still resolute despite her situation—people with her kind of mental fortitude really were different. This was in a different league from my conversation with Sengoku the day before yesterday.

"An aberration…"

An aberration.

There was a reason for an aberration.

"Yes…which is why," Hanekawa said, looking at me, "I was hoping you could take me to Mister Oshino's place… He still lives in that abandoned cram school, doesn't he? I know that much, but I just couldn't figure out how to get there—"

"……"

It wasn't that she didn't know.

She'd forgotten.

The place had gone under, so a map could only help so much… Maybe it wasn't impossible if she unearthed an old map, but it would take too long, and time was of the essence here. She must have decided that sending me an SOS was faster.

"Could you show me the way?" she requested.

"Yeah, of course—"

I had no reason to say no.

Although Oshino was probably asleep at this hour of the morning and we'd be interrupting his slumber, that wasn't something I needed to be bringing up. He tended to wake up on the wrong side of bed, maybe because of low blood pressure or something…but we had to do this anyway.

"—Of course," I said, "but could I ask you a few questions first?"

"Um…sure, but why?"

"I'm constantly relying on Oshino when it comes to every little thing relating to aberrations. We need to keep on trying to do as much as we can by ourselves. Even if we end up dumping the whole thing onto him, we should at least get the story straight before we do."

"Oh… Yes, you're right." Hanekawa sounded convinced. "Okay, ask me anything you want."

"You had headaches, right? You said you've been having a lot of them lately, but when exactly did they start?"

"When exactly…"

"You would remember."

"…About a month ago, I guess? Hm, but while they weren't so bad at first…yesterday and the day before—I was with you both times, at the bookstore and in front of school—they were actually pretty bad."

"You should've told me."

"Sorry. I didn't want you to worry."

"Whatever, it's fine. Okay, then… Did you have any episodes involving cats after Golden Week?"

"Episodes involving cats?"

"Even something like a black cat crossing your path."

"……"

Hanekawa closed her eyes and made a show of sifting through her memories.

Frankly, I wasn't sure if it was the kind of thing you could remember if you tried…but then again, she was "the real deal" who lived in a different world, even according to Senjogahara…

Try to apply common sense to her and you'd end up hurt.

Which is *precisely why*—she was visited by an aberration.

"On the night of May twenty-seventh, I was listening to a radio program when a message by one 'Bearcat Lover' was read on the air.

Could that have something to do with it?"

"...No, I don't think so."

Oh my god.

I knew, but oh my god.

"By the way, the letter went, 'While maids are shown leading fun and carefree lives in manga and anime, being a maid is a surprisingly difficult job. It's not all about being cute and saying 'moé moé!' From what I understand, they barely have any time to themselves. I'm sure of it, because that's what I was told the other day at a mixer.'"

"Really, you don't have to explain all that!"

"What do you think is so interesting about that letter, Araragi? I had a hard time understanding."

"Um, it's supposed to be funny because the maid says there's barely any time she has to herself when she's off at a fun and carefree mixer, meeting guys—and why do I have to fill in the gaps that this 'Bearcat Lover' left in the story for you?!"

"Oh, so when it said 'told the other day at a mixer,' it means told by a maid. I see, it might be amusing if you interpret it that way. But I do think it's a bit hard to understand if you only get to hear it once."

"And now that I think about it, bearcats aren't cats, they're more like civets."

"Yes, I guess you're right."

"Anything else?"

"Hm? Anything else? Well, there was one 'Oracle's Auricle' on the same program. 'A little while back, I was playing cards with two friends and we decided to play President. After we dealt out the cards, one of my friends said something. "So at my middle school, we played with a rule where 4's were the highest card."' This was a listener's corner so I imagine it was a true story, but what's so funny about it?"

"No, when I asked you if you had anything else, I didn't mean other listener letters that you couldn't find the humor in! But well, you have to listen to that story knowing that President has a lot of local variants, whether that means 8's are played as the highest card or that if Presidents fail to keep their position they automatically become the asshole. You're supposed to laugh because the friend used the existence of all these variants as an excuse to make up a rule that would make his hand better!"

"Oh, I see. I can always count on you, Araragi."

"You can be as impressed as you want, but I'm not going to take it as a compliment… Oh, and I guess the handle 'Oracle's Auricle' is also a little joke in that it might actually be 'Oracle's Oracle' or even 'Auricle's Oracle' but you wouldn't know for sure."

"Oh, but it's not as if every letter they read on that program is hard to understand. Some of them are regular, funny letters. There was another true story during that same listener's corner from 'Ain't Nothin' Like a Found Dog.' 'I went to a video rental store the other day with my friend. I wanted to borrow the DVDs for this drama series that aired about three years ago, but someone else had rented volume eight of a set of thirteen, so I could only get up to volume seven. I was disappointed because I'd heard the end of the series is its best part. It was only that eighth volume that they didn't have, while nine through thirteen were all there on the shelf. When I told my friend, "It's like I'm playing Sevens and I've been cut off at the eights," my friend replied, "I bet whoever has volume eight is chuckling right now."' Haha, get it? Because whoever has volume eight doesn't see it as playing Sevens at all!"

"I'll admit that might be funny, but enough about the radio!"

But we digressed.

Anyway.

If that was all she could come up with in the way of memories relating to cats, maybe we should consider the current case to be last time's leftovers?

We probably should.

"All right, Hanekawa. Next question."

"Okay."

"That hat," I said. "Would you take it off for me?"

"…That's—" Hanekawa's expression changed. "That's not a question, Araragi."

"No, it isn't."

"I know it's not."

"Miss Hanekawa. Allow me to take your hat for you."

"Araragi."

"Yes?"

"You're going to make me mad."

"Then be mad," I said, not faltering despite Hanekawa's threatening glare. "If you want to get mad, get mad. You can even hate me if you want, I don't care. Paying back what I owe you is a lot more important to me than our friendship."

"Paying me back? What…" Hanekawa's voice grew a bit softer, as if my words had made her feel awkward. "What are you talking about?"

"I'm talking about spring break."

"That's—but that was just… That, if anything, was a case of just going and getting saved on your own—no?"

"No. Oshino might say so, but I think you saved me. You saved my life."

It felt like I'd finally been able to say it.

Right.

If either of us needed to properly thank the other—then I did.

"I don't think I can ever pay you back in full," I told her. "But I want you to let me do something for you. I'll do anything, everything for you. And if you get mad or hate me in the process, so be it."

"So be it, huh?" Hanekawa laughed—just a little.

No, perhaps she cried.

I couldn't tell.

"Oh, get over yourself," she said.

"Really?"

"This is you we're talking about, Araragi. Do you really think you're so great?"

"…That line belongs to some neighborhood bully."

And not to a model student.

Yes, you're right, Hanekawa said, and then—"Don't laugh."

She took off her hat.

"..
...."

She had cat ears.

A pair of cute cat ears protruded from Hanekawa's little head.

I bit my lip in silence.

So hard that blood began to ooze from it.

…Don't laugh…

I'd just acted serious in getting her to do this. I mustn't laugh… I'd finally gotten her to agree after crafting the most serious and solemn excuse I could come up with. It'd be a textbook manga gag if I burst into laughter and ridiculed her, but I swore that I wouldn't…

Still, the cat ears went well on her. It was as if they were tailor-made to go along with her neat and straight bangs. A thought I first had during Golden Week came back to me: she'd been born to wear a pair of cat ears on her head someday…

That said.

During the Golden Week nightmare, it was never *Hanekawa as herself with cat ears*—so she was blowing me away now. I see, I thought, so the color of the fur on her ears *in this case* was black, the same as her hair…

It still was no excuse to laugh.

She really would hate me then.

I'd said I wouldn't mind if she did, but I preferred to avoid that outcome at the end of the day. It's depressing to be hated by a decent person who even saved your life.

"A-Are we done?"

Hanekawa sounded embarrassed.

It was rare to see her cheeks so tinged with color.

And she had cat ears!

"Oh, yeah…sure. Thanks."

"Why are you thanking me?" she said, putting her hat back on. She wore it deep and avoided my eyes. It was similar to when Kanbaru showed me her left arm or when Sengoku showed us her body…but Hanekawa's cat ears were on a different plane.

To the point where I wanted to thank her.

Thank you so much.

"Well…okay, I think I get it," I said. "It really is like we're *picking up* where Golden Week left off. So I guess it wasn't all over…"

The headaches must have been from the ears growing on her head.

Easy enough to understand if you thought of it that way.

Like wisdom teeth growing in.

"Picking up where Golden Week left off?" asked Hanekawa. "So you mean—the stuff I forgot."

"You're better off forgetting."

"Yes, I'm sure...but I don't know, it just feels so unpleasant to have a hole in my memory. Like I'm lacking whatever ought to be there."

It wasn't a lack that she was feeling.

It was probably—loss.

"Don't take it the wrong way, but I'm a little relieved," I said. "If that's the problem—there's a way to deal with it. You might not remember, but I went through this once already. All we have to do is repeat what we did, and this will be settled. Only this time, we'll be thorough, through and through."

"Oh—is that so."

Hanekawa was visibly less tense now that she heard this.

Well, of course she'd panic. Who wouldn't if they woke up with cat ears sprouting out of their head—even if she recovered some of her memories in the process? You couldn't blame her for leaping out of the house still in her pajamas.

In such situations—

Hanekawa couldn't stay cooped up at home.

"Okay," I said. "Now that we've sorted things out, why don't we head to Oshino's place... You're not gonna tell me that riding two to a bicycle is against traffic laws, are you?"

"As much as I'd like to," Hanekawa replied standing up from the bench, "I'll overlook it. But we're even for me getting you to skip school."

Wait, how did that make it even?

Both of them were her call. She could be surprisingly cunning at times...

Actually, it must have been her idea of a joke.

Or maybe you could call it her way of hiding her embarrassment.

"Shall I lend you my shoulder? You seem tired."

"I'm fine. Remember, I said my headache's gone. I'm emotionally exhausted right now, but that's all. My body feels better than usual, if anything."

"Does it now."

Well, she was a cat.

It was the same with Kanbaru's monkey.

We walked to the bike parking and unlocked my bicycle and got on, me first on the saddle, then her on the back seat.

Hanekawa's arms wrapped around my torso, then squeezed.

Her body was now stuck to mine.

"………"

Ack…

They were so soft!

And so big!

The two sensations I felt on my back mercilessly assailed my heart, whipping it into a frenzy… I confess, it was such a shock that I'm sure I'd have lost control if she'd been anyone but Tsubasa Hanekawa, the girl I owed my life to, and if I didn't have a girlfriend, and also if that girlfriend weren't Hitagi Senjogahara.

Tsubasa Hanekawa was a girl with hidden assets.

Yes, it was hard to see thanks to the utterly plain appearance she put forward, following the school dress code to a T, but she had an incredible body… I'd come to learn that more than well enough over Golden Week. Senjogahara had sat on the very same back seat, but aware as she was, she'd used her innate sense of balance to barely touch me…

And we weren't even going out then.

Meanwhile, Tsubasa Hanekawa's morals and ethics stood no chance in the face of her devoted adherence to traffic safety. She entrusted her entire body to me, making the situation, quite frankly, no laughing matter.

Plus, I'd been wearing my high-collared school jacket with Senjogahara. Now that I was wearing my summer uniform, I was in a short-sleeved button-down. This difference was, practically speaking, a pretty big one. But was that all it took for them to feel this soft? As far as summer uniforms went, I was in mine the day before yesterday when Sengoku sat behind me, too… Well, there was the more basic issue of Sengoku's body not protruding much in any direction, but still.

And then I realized. Oh. Right, just as I wasn't wearing anything under my button-down, she was only wearing her pajamas under that light blouse... Miss Hanekawa, are you not wearing a bra?

Oh, wow...

So these kinds of things really happen over the course of your life...

"Araragi."

"Hm?"

"We need to talk once we get off this bike."

"........."

The words sent a chill down my spine.

She saw straight through me...

I was so shallow.

"Well, uh," I stammered. "Putting that aside, let's go. Hold on tight so that you don't fall off..."

Hey!

I was trying to get myself out of it, why was I digging myself in deeper?!

I couldn't find my rhythm!

While I was busy throwing myself to the sharks, Hanekawa stayed quiet.

Too quiet.

She wasn't saying a word.

"O-Okay, here we go."

In the end, all I could do was coweringly announce our departure before beginning to turn the pedals. With the weight of two people on my bike, they felt that much heavier. The standard routine here would have been the classic "You're heavier than I thought" and Hanekawa getting mad, but I decided to pass.

Plus, she wasn't what I'd call heavy.

It wouldn't take too long to get to the abandoned cram school where Oshino and Shinobu lived—an hour or less if I went as fast as I could, even with two people... Something incredible happened on my back every time we hit a bump in the road, but I chose to pay as little attention as possible to the fact. I wasn't going to intentionally steer us over any bumps on the asphalt, I was a gentleman. Well, then again, I

117

wasn't sure—even if I didn't intentionally go over any bumps, might I not merely fail to avoid whatever bumps presented themselves on our way and still call myself a gentleman?

"It must be hard for you," Hanekawa said to me after a while—after starting to get used to what must have been her first time riding two to a bike, or at least her first time since she was six. "Looking after so many people in so many different ways."

"So many people? What do you mean?"

"Like Senjogahara, or Mayoi, or Kanbaru, or that junior high girl from yesterday, Sengoku... Haha, they're all girls."

"Oh, shut it."

"And every time—it had to do with aberrations. I remember now."

By "remember," I assumed she meant something like "connect the dots."

"It's still a little fuzzy, but...yeah. There's no way Senjogahara would have gotten over her illness so suddenly..."

"..."

"So it started when you were attacked by a vampire over spring break... It all started from there."

"Aberrations themselves are always there, like a part of nature—it's not as if they appear out of nowhere one day. Apparently."

At least according to Mèmè Oshino, the expert.

"Did you know, Araragi?"

"Did I know what?"

"There's a special trait that vampires have—fascination. They can use it to charm humans."

"Charm?"

I didn't exactly know what she was getting at. Um...was it their ability to suck blood to increase their numbers? Like Shinobu did to me?

When I asked her, she shook her head.

"Uh-uh."

I could tell she was shaking her head no by the way it moved along my back.

"That's their most famous trait. This is similar, but a little different... It doesn't involve sucking blood. If anything is like hypnosis, maybe that's it... Looking into someone else's eyes allows them to enthrall the opposite sex. Though I'm not sure if 'the opposite sex' is the right term here, since vampires and humans belong to different species."

"Huh. Okay, so what about that?"

"Nothing. I was just thinking." Hanekawa's voice was quieter now. "Maybe that's why you've been so popular with girls lately."

"......"

Fascination.

A special vampire trait.

Ah. I may not have been a vampire anymore, but it was still entirely possible. It wasn't like I was a dating-sim protagonist like Hachikuji and I had discussed earlier...but that was a realistic justification for what was happening.

That's Hanekawa for you.

She saw things in a different way.

But—it'd be awful if that's what it was.

I mean, if that were true, wouldn't that change everything about my relationship with Hitagi Senjogahara—

And all that fun I had talking to Hachikuji—

And how attached Kanbaru was to me—

And even Sengoku, too—

"...Sorry," Hanekawa said. "That was mean of me, wasn't it."

"Not really—I wouldn't say so. Actually, it all makes more sense to me now. Of course. Up until last year, I pretty much didn't have a single friend if you think about it—yeah, I can remember those days when my phone's contact list didn't have one entry on it..."

I could memorize every number I needed.

It was a little too hard for that now.

"Huh, fascination," I grunted. "Okay. You really know everything, don't you?"

"I don't know everything," answered Hanekawa. "I don't. I don't know anything."

"........."

Huh?

That didn't sound like her normal line?

But before I could voice my doubts, she continued, "You were already a vampire when you met me over spring break—weren't you."

"Yeah. I was right in the middle of it. I wasn't a mockery but an authentic, genuine, full-fledged vampire then. Heh, so I guess you might've also been fascinated by me after all—ow!"

Hanekawa had squeezed her arms tighter around my torso.

Wasn't that a sumo move? A *sabaori*, I think?!

"No, Araragi. A sabaori, or a forward force down, is done from the front. Also, it's used to bring an opponent to his knees, not to crush his internal organs."

"Oh, okay. You're really well-inform—wait, crush my internal organs?!"

Hanekawa had just said something I'd expect to hear from Senjogahara!

Women are terrifying!

What if Hanekawa realized that her move wasn't that effective thanks to the two large cushions on my back?!

Well, it was my fault.

I wasn't paying attention and had said something inappropriate.

Hanekawa must have been in a fairly uneasy state of mind—she'd half-regained her memories, and now she was thinking about all sorts of things she normally wouldn't to make up for all that was lacking and lost.

I couldn't blame her if her head wasn't in the right place.

I'd been impressed a little earlier by how Hanekawa calculated everything out from my attendance to prepping for the culture festival. But when I thought about it some more, if all she wanted was to get to the abandoned cram school where Oshino lived, it could have been handled via texting. She only had to ask me for directions—there was no need to get me to skip school and summon me all the way to that distant park.

Yet she had.

And not because her head wasn't in the right place.

It must have been because she felt uneasy.

If I'd figured it out with enough time, Hanekawa would have

noticed immediately—so it wasn't as if she hadn't. She was just too afraid to face an aberration alone.

That made me glad.

I probably wouldn't be any help to her at all yet again—the only option seemed to be to ask Mèmè Oshino and Shinobu Oshino to deal with this cat aberration. There was nothing I could do for her. I could say I'd do everything for her—but from the start, that was nothing at all.

Even then, I could be by her side.

The simple fact of being there when you're needed is enough. There's nothing more you have to do to earn someone's gratitude—as Daddy Senjogahara put it.

If that was the case, the one person who was there for me when I needed it the most was none other than Tsubasa Hanekawa.

That's why I'd decided.

Even if there wasn't a thing I could do, I'd be there for Hanekawa when she needed it, no matter what—

I don't ever change, after all.

Hanekawa had said that to me yesterday.

But really, I thought, there's nothing that never changes—and from my point of view, Hanekawa had actually changed, and quite a bit.

She'd changed—ever since getting involved with an aberration.

The biggest example being the post-graduation plans she'd shared with me at the bookstore.

She'd take two years or so—and wander the world.

She was going on a journey.

Hanekawa would never have chosen such a fantastic path for herself, at least not the Hanekawa I knew until the end of last school year—she'd been traveling along the hammered-out, conventional set of rails for a model student like herself.

This isn't to pass judgment about right or wrong paths—but there was the simple fact that Tsubasa Hanekawa had changed. Whether it was after the end of Golden Week or after spring break—that was something I didn't know.

But.

From there, Hanekawa and I continued without talking about

much else until we arrived at the cram school that had grown derelict a few years ago and was now serving as Oshino and Shinobu's den. A tattered fence snaked around this building that could only be described as dilapidated. "No Trespassing" signs were scattered all around the structure, making the two squatters. How many times have I come to this place over the last three months, I wondered. I realized that I'd become completely used to visiting it. Aberrations were no longer something out of the ordinary for me—

"Oh? Why, if it isn't you, Araragi."

Suddenly.

I heard this voice ahead of me.

"And missy class president...right? I tend to have trouble keeping track of who women are when they change their hairstyle, but from the glasses I'm sure that's missy class president. Ha hah, it's been a while, class prez. And Araragi, it's been a day."

It was Mèmè Oshino.

There on the other side of the ripped fence stood a middle-aged man in a psychedelic Hawaiian shirt, looking aloof. He looked as shabby as ever, but I also realized it had been the first time in a while I'd seen him doing something outside the building. What was he up to? I thought he was supposed to be a weird kind of shut-in who refused to leave his ruins.

"Hmm..." I mused. "Wait, you always say something like 'I've been waiting for you' or 'You kept me waiting for long enough' when I see you, like you saw it all coming. You're not going to do that this time?"

"Oh... Huh? Do I?"

Oshino was acting somehow unnatural.

"Missy class president," he continued as if to dodge the question, switching his attention to Hanekawa who stood behind my bike. "It really has been a while, hasn't it, class prez. What's the matter? Isn't today a weekday? Araragi's one thing, but I couldn't imagine you ever playing hooky. Ha hah, I know, it's one of those School Foundation Days I've heard so much about, isn't it?"

"Oh, um... No, it isn't."

"Hm? You look good in a hat—like that one on your head," Oshino immediately zeroed in on Hanekawa's headgear.

When it came to this kind of thing—you could tell he was a pro.

"…Thank you."

Oshino returned his attention to me. "Huh—so that's how it is, Araragi?"

His expression was lax—the same Oshino as ever.

"You really can't go three steps without attracting trouble, can you—that's actually a talent, in a sense. Maybe you ought to cherish it. Ha hah, well come on in for now. So, Araragi—actually, I'm in the middle of something for once. I'm busy and don't have much time."

"Oh—really?"

In the middle of something?

Busy?

He didn't have time?

None of those things sounded natural coming from Oshino's mouth.

"Were you—in the middle of work?"

"Well, you could call it work if you wanted. But it's fine. You're one thing, Araragi, but I can be flexible if it's something serious with missy president."

"You're being really dismissive of me today…"

"What, do you want me to like you? You're creeping me out, how unpleasant."

Oshino shooed me away with a cold gesture.

My vampire fascination didn't seem to work on him, at least… Oh, but if it was the power to enthrall the opposite sex, I guess it only worked on the opposite sex.

"Now stop complaining about nothing and get yourself inside, both of you. Come in through that hole in the fence over there. We'll talk on the fourth floor, like always."

"Yeah… Fine," I said.

I did as told.

In any case, thanks to Oshino being outside, I escaped getting chewed out by Hanekawa the moment we got off my bike. It may have been a godsend, but I was dealing with Hanekawa and her miraculous powers of retention. I couldn't rejoice over being spared; I'd only delayed my inevitable lecture. In fact, I almost started to feel depressed when I realized I might end up accruing interest on that chewing-out in the meantime.

We entered through the fence and pushed our way into the ruins through the vegetation that now grew everywhere with summer approaching. The mess inside the building was still part of Hanekawa's memories, so she said nothing about it. It may sound like a nasty joke, but Hanekawa really did look at Oshino with respect, making her excessively lenient when it came to all he did that made him unfit to live in society.

That's right.

Tsubasa Hanekawa's post-graduation path that you could barely call a path, the idea of wandering the world, owed more than a little to Mèmè Oshino, who tread an unblazed trail. Not that it meant anything in the end since Hanekawa had ultimately made that choice for herself, but—

I still had my thoughts.

"A *Sawarineko*. An Afflicting Cat."

Oshino said the words—as we climbed the stairs.

A cat.

A mammal belonging to Carnivora Felidae.

Notable for their flexible bodies, sharp teeth, coarse tongues, and claws—they say cats hide their claws, and there's a reason for that, which is the sheaths they store them in. The soft pads on their paws that humans love to touch play a practical role, too, muffling the sound of their footsteps when hunting prey.

"Also known as a Silver Cat. They're also called Dancing Cats, but not often, due to another creature with the same name. Yes, Sawarineko would be the customary name. An affliction that is a cat, or an Afflicting Cat. Sawarineko. A cat with no tail—a cat that leaves no trail. An aberration. It's said that cats entered Japan in the Nara period, during the eighth century. It's well-known they were once used to make *shamisen* guitars, but—yes, cats are now entirely pets, even more so than dogs. They don't catch mice. You never hear of police cats or seeing-eye cats.

If we were to discuss Japanese legends involving cats, we would have to mention the three famed tales of *bakeneko*, Changing Cats... Ha hah, well, you may be one thing, Araragi, but I'm sure this all goes without saying for you, missy class prez?"

"Hey, Oshino. Stop saying 'You're one thing, Araragi' like it's some sort of refrain whenever you talk about Hanekawa. It's actually starting to get to me."

"Well, it's not like I'm doing it intentionally, but the truth tends to slip out of people's mouths."

"You'd better watch out next time you're out walking at night."

"No need to worry, I'm nocturnal. Ha hah, and I guess cats are, too," he noted as we reached the fourth floor.

Hanekawa spoke less and less as we walked up the stairs. And just like Oshino said, Hanekawa shouldn't need any explanations about this aberration—the exact same words had come out of his mouth during Golden Week.

But—were *those memories* still there?

It might have been Oshino's way of checking. Mèmè Oshino was a man who never seemed to be thinking anything but usually was.

We entered the classroom.

First Oshino, then me, then Hanekawa—

Then Oshino went back to close the door.

The classroom was reasonably bright. It was the afternoon, and sunlight was coming in through the windows (though I hesitate to call frames with odd shards of glass sticking out of them windows).

Hmm...Shinobu wasn't around.

It seemed like she wasn't on the fourth floor very much these days... Oh, and I was forgetting because of Hanekawa, but I needed to bring up what Hachikuji had told me about Shinobu yesterday...if Hachikuji indeed saw what she thought she saw—

And then.

I turned around at almost the exact moment Oshino took Hanekawa by surprise and tapped her through her hat from above.

It was only a tap.

And yet—Hanekawa crumpled.

She fell to her knees and slumped over, her face to the floor.

Like her strings had been cut.

"H-Hanekawa?!"

"Don't get so worked up, Araragi. You're spirited today. Something good happen to you? Like you got to see missy class president's cat ears, or maybe her in her pajamas?"

"No tacking on actual guesses to your catchphrase! She'll get the wrong idea!"

"There's nothing wrong about it. In fact, you ought to be thanking me for ignoring for all this time how missy class prez was on the back seat of your bike and holding her arms around you." He was looking down at Hanekawa as she lay collapsed on the floor. "And it seems to me that you've already gotten her story—look at you, you're learning. Almost like that experience with missies tsundere, lost girl, sapphy, and bashful wasn't all wasted on you. And missy bashful's case the day before yesterday seems to have made an especially big impact on you."

So Sengoku had become Bashful.

That didn't seem like enough to describe her, but...

Whatever, there was no need to correct him.

There was something more pressing.

I asked Oshino, "Anyway...what'd you do to Hanekawa?"

"Like I said, thanks to the lessons you've learned, there was barely anything I had to do. I skipped a few steps."

"You did what?"

What did that mean?

Could he do that?

"Though I'd call it heterodox. There's no time—that's what you said, right? And in this case...as I think you know well enough, it'd be much quicker to have a *direct discussion* than to go through missy class prez."

"...So you want to go direct."

"We can grill her all we want, *but no matter how much of her memory has returned, she still doesn't remember*—we won't get anywhere. I understand that you might feel upset because I hit a girl on the head when she wasn't expecting it, but this wouldn't have worked without the element of surprise. Okay? Your forgiveness, please."

But it was tough finding an opening, this girl never lets her guard down—Oshino said.

Well, that's Hanekawa for you.

So Oshino had been watching Hanekawa and searching for his "opening" this whole time?

"You said a direct discussion…"

"I don't think there's any need to explain. Let's do a good job here, Araragi. We're going to be facing off against someone as smart as missy class president. If we aren't prepared ourselves—well, even I was taken by surprise over Golden Week. But we're not going to make that mistake again. And speak of the devil, she's here already, Araragi. The lust-besotted cat has made her appearance."

Then, when I looked at her.

Even as Hanekawa lay there facedown on the floor, her long hair, normally tied in braids—began to change color.

It changed color.

No—it lost color.

It went from a solid black to a near-white silver.

As if all life were being drained from it.

"………"

No words.

I had somewhat of a feeling *this* would happen from the moment we went to visit Oshino, and I thought I'd prepared myself to a degree— even so, I couldn't hide how shaken I felt now that I'd been *reunited* with her so suddenly.

I really was flimsy.

Flimsy and weak.

I was going to be there for Hanekawa when she needed me, no matter what—wasn't that the promise I'd made?

Then, lunging—

She leapt to her feet.

The hat flew from her head from the momentum.

It flew away—exposing them.

Her white hair, cut in straight bangs.

The pair of white cat ears protruding from her little head.

"Myaa-hahaha!"

And then—

She narrowed her eyes like a cat and flashed me a catlike grin.

"What a surpurrrise. I never thought we'd meet again, human—and I see ya still haven't learned, ya bad little kitty. Getting aroused by my myaster's breasts, you're so purrsistent. Trying to get yourself eaten alive?"

"………"

A single outburst that succinctly conveyed her character traits and positioning—

It marked the second coming of Black Hanekawa.

006

It feels like there's no need to go into a flashback after Black Hanekawa gave such a beginner-friendly explanation of herself, but allow me to invite you to the first day of Golden Week anyway, April twenty-ninth, one morning about a month and a half earlier, in part to help set the stage. Back in the days when my hair was still at a vague and uneasy length as I grew it out to hide the bite marks on my neck.

April twenty-ninth.

Morning.

As someone who hates any day that isn't a regular weekday, I left the house and was wandering around as usual on this holiday, riding around town on my mountain bike, still going strong in those days before Kanbaru destroyed it. Unlike Mother's Day, it felt as if I had a clear destination, but I don't remember very well. And even if I did, the fact that I've forgotten it means it couldn't have been that important.

No.

It meant that what ended up happening while I was on the road—was just too big.

Personally speaking.

So big that everything else ceased to matter.

I just so happened—to come across Hanekawa.

I first got to know Hanekawa over spring break—as I've said many times up until now, it was then she'd saved me.

Both physically and mentally.

I was more grateful for the latter at the time, as I was immortal—but in any case, she was my savior.

She'd saved my life, and she'd saved my mind.

She'd been there when I needed her to be.

That's what I think.

I really do.

About as much as I'm glad that I happened to be standing on the landing that day Senjogahara slipped on the stairs—I'm really, truly glad that it was her, Tsubasa Hanekawa, there at that moment, and not anyone else.

Anyone else and I'd never have been saved.

I'd have never been released from hell.

Hanekawa and I ended up in the same class after spring break. She forced me into the position of class vice president. She put me under her management because of her mistaken assumption that I was a delinquent, and that was her way of rehabilitating me. There isn't any way she was planning to help me with my studies at the time—and normally I'd have shoved her away and told her to get her nose out of my business. There's nothing I dislike more than people who seem to impose on me because of a big, fat misunderstanding.

But I accepted it.

Because she was Hanekawa.

So after that—over the month of April—Hanekawa and I, as class president, as class vice president, and as class president and vice president, began to get along to some degree as we made arrangements for school events and class matters. I hadn't done anything that felt like it in a while, and I found myself getting uncharacteristically into it—so, of course.

If I saw Hanekawa walking around in her uniform on a holiday, I'd say hello to her at least.

It was the normal thing to do.

But I flinched for a moment.

A large white piece of gauze concealed what felt like half of Tsubasa Hanekawa's face as she walked there on the street.

An injury.

Everyone gets injured.

But an injury to the face, as well as an injury of that scale—that was a rare sight. There was also the fact that the gauze was over the left side of her face—there seemed to be a story behind it.

Maybe I was overthinking things.

It could have been that my violent spring break was driving me to brutal thoughts. Most people are right-handed, and if they were to hit someone else in the face, their fist would land on the left side of that face—those kinds of thoughts. But even if I didn't think of it like that—how could you manage to hurt just that part of your body and nowhere else? Hanekawa, a third-year, couldn't have decided to throw herself into some after-school sport the day before—

But as I was thinking.

Hanekawa noticed me back.

"Oh," she said, approaching me. Her attitude was as friendly as ever. "Howdy, Araragi."

"…Howdy."

"Hm? Oh."

And then.

Hanekawa looked as though she'd failed at something.

Now that I look back at it, it seems unbelievable—for any regular person, maybe it couldn't be helped, but you could call it a major blunder from Hanekawa, the master tactician.

Or no, maybe you could call it a success.

And if you did, a major success.

After all, Hanekawa would have been trying, trying so hard, trying so desperately hard not to think of the gauze on her face—and so.

Calling out to me like nothing was amiss, without worrying about the gauze, like it was another day, was a major success worthy of the "real" Hanekawa.

But, of course.

It was a failure when you looked at the big picture.

I tried to gloss over this—I pretended not to notice Hanekawa's failure and want to say I asked her about something stupid. The same kind of stupid that I treated her to every time we'd met over the past month. Hanekawa always went along with it.

But.

She just couldn't that day.

"You're so kind, Araragi," she said. "You're such a good and kind person."

That's right.

I was told this—back on that day, too.

Hanekawa had.

"Let's walk. Just for a little," she invited me.

I had no reason to say no.

Well, I wouldn't have ever said no. Hanekawa had never invited me to do something like that before—I'd say she must have wanted company.

She couldn't bear being alone.

She didn't invite me because it was me, it could have been anyone.

It just so happened to be me there at that moment.

I probably wasn't the best person for the situation from Hanekawa's point of view—I doubt she'd have chosen me had she been the slightest bit calm. Unlike Mayoi Hachikuji, whom I'd come to meet later, I wasn't what anyone would describe as a good listener. I'm too quick to become emotionally involved, I can't keep my mouth shut when I'm being talked to, and I interrupt other people's stories all the time.

But Hanekawa was a good enough talker to make up for all of that and more, and was able to take it without much issue. Pushing my bike, I walked alongside her and listened to her talk.

First off.

Tsubasa Hanekawa doesn't have a father.

Yes, biologically speaking she'd have to have a father, but socially speaking she was born to a mother who was entirely on her own. Hanekawa still didn't know her father's whereabouts. She had no interest in trying to find out more, but even if she did, she most likely would have arrived at a guess at best, nothing with any degree of certainty.

Tsubasa.

The name she'd been given—"wing."

The character "Tsubasa" has connotations of covering and aiding, as in a bird using its wing to protect its eggs or chicks—

Taking under one's wing.

That thought didn't come to me at the time, though.

But—shouldn't the person who named her have been the one aiding her at that moment? What could her mother have possibly been thinking when she gave her that name?

What kind of task had she given her daughter?

She apparently had a different last name at the time.

I didn't ask what it was.

Well, it was more like I couldn't ask.

Hanekawa tried to tell me, but I stopped her. *Yes,* she understood right away and continued her story.

Hanekawa's mother had her, then married right afterwards.

She was getting married for the first time.

In any case—it sounds like she needed the money. Raising Hanekawa on her own must have been tough. This all happened nearly twenty years ago, so the social welfare system must not have been as robust then, either. Even I could imagine how tough it would have been for a single mother and a single child to live on their own without anyone's help.

A mother.

A father.

But, right after the marriage—her mother committed suicide.

She'd married for money, and the marriage had failed in no time at all. It sounds like she was in a delicate emotional state from the beginning. Like she was the kind of person who found living with others to be agonizing—turning Hanekawa into a single child with a single mother into a single child with a single father.

A father she wasn't related to by blood.

But still, her father.

This father's last name—wasn't Hanekawa, either.

And I couldn't ask for that name, either.

Not much time after her mother's suicide, this father, unrelated by blood, decided to remarry. Hanekawa wasn't yet at the age where she felt any particular way about this—but as a result she was in a three-person family once again. She now found herself unrelated by blood to both of her parents.

I didn't know how I was supposed to feel about that.

Was it that unfortunate of a situation?

Was I supposed to pity Hanekawa?

It didn't do to declare her unfortunate simply because her life hadn't followed a more conventional path—true, her birth mother had ended her life in an unfortunate way, but that unhappiness didn't necessarily latch itself onto Hanekawa. Indeed, you could say she was fortunate to have a father who took her in and to have found herself with a new mother.

A lot of things had happened to her—

That didn't mean on its own that her life was unfortunate.

So even if her father died from overwork after that, and she became a single child with a single mother again, only to find herself with another new father a year later, at last making her name "Hanekawa"—my opinion on the matter ought to stay the same.

It didn't make sense to pity her.

We might feel bad for her first mother and the first father who died, but only those two. No one else.

Still, what a tumultuous life.

At that point, Hanekawa had yet to turn three—she was at an age where she didn't understand anything yet. Yes, all she could do was go with the flow, no matter how ludicrous that flow may have been.

I'd misunderstood.

Good people like Hanekawa must have been blessed, I thought.

They must be loved by the gods, I thought.

I'd had the impression until then that good people were fortunate, and that bad people were unfortunate—but that's not how it is.

Spending time with my family on holidays felt suffocating, so I'd leave the house. I lived the kind of life where worries as lukewarm as that counted as worries. But when it came to complicated family situations—

Hers was worlds apart.

It sounded so fake it was almost comical. I wouldn't have believed it if anyone other than Hanekawa had told me—I'd have laughed them off. But I was at a loss for words because it was Hanekawa, someone who I knew would never tell such a crass joke. And so, after all the back and forth, she came to have two parents with no relation whatsoever to her.

A single mother and a single child.

A step, step, step—child.

"Sorry," Hanekawa finished. She was apologizing to me. "That was mean of me, wasn't it."

How did I reply then?

Was I able to say—"Not really"?

Nope.

I asked her, *Why? What are you talking about?*

It was like I was forcing a confession out of her. How dense could I be? For someone as earnest as Hanekawa, it must have sounded like an accusation.

"Well, I'm just venting at you," she said. "What are you supposed to say in this situation, right? You'd wonder, 'Okay, so what,' it's not like it has anything to do with you in the first place—but then you start to feel a little pity for me until you feel guilty for pitying me when it doesn't make sense to, right? You...felt bad just now, like you did something wrong, didn't you?"

She'd nailed it.

It was mean of me, she said.

"I used you to cheer myself up."

"......"

"I tried to feel better about myself by making you feel bad—I can't even call it griping."

It was the first time I'd ever seen Hanekawa so despondent.

The gauze on her face might have been adding to it.

My image of Tsubasa Hanekawa was of someone who stood firm and upright, who was strong, who was earnest—who was reliable, wise, fair—who was perfect.

But.

There's no such thing as a perfect person.

"Still—I'm surprised you know all that," I said. "Don't they usually not tell kids about that kind of thing? Like, they'll keep it a secret until your twentieth birthday or something."

"Well, I had some very open parents. I knew about it from before I started elementary school," Hanekawa said, still walking at the same pace. "I really do feel like I'm in their way."

"......"

"But at the same time, they do have to consider how society sees them. You can't toss your child away because your partner dies, and you can't toss your child away because you're getting remarried, either. I hear she tried to put me in a home—in the end, though, she didn't feel like she could take people criticizing her because she let go of a very young child for her own selfish reasons."

"........."

What was I supposed to say to that? But.

It happened, even in families related by blood. In fact, you could say it's rare to find a family where everything is smooth sailing—all families hide some kind of discord and strain.

"That's why I tried to become a good girl," Hanekawa said. "I tried to become a serious class president ever since I was in elementary school—and I guess I have. What a well-behaved kid I am, ha ha."

Those words—remind me of what I'd hear later about Hitagi Senjogahara's life. Hitagi Senjogahara in middle school, and Hitagi Senjogahara in high school—

Is that what it meant? That they shared more than a hairstyle?

But the differences between them were just as clear.

Because parents might be responsible for what their children do—but children don't bear any responsibility at all for what their parents do.

"Maybe not a good girl. A normal girl." Hanekawa continued as I kept silent. "People see it as some kind of trauma when you have a complicated family situation and assume all these things about you because of that, you know? I didn't want people to think of me that way. That's why—I decided I wasn't going to let something like that change me."

I don't ever change.

136

No matter what.

"I was being a normal high school student, yes?"

"No…I'm not so sure about that one."

Normal high school students don't get the highest scores on national mock exams.

They can't live such impeccable, irreproachable lives.

I'd meant it half-jokingly, as a way to clear the air, but—

"Maybe you're right," Hanekawa said with disappointment in her voice. "Maybe it does seep out in the end—maybe you can tell when people who aren't normal force themselves to act like they are. Maybe they overdo it."

"That's not a bad thing—is it? It only means you're living a better life."

"No, it doesn't. I mean, how typical. *Because of her birth, because of her upbringing—she's now such a good and well-behaved girl.*"

Bouncing back from your misfortune to work hard.

Bouncing back from adversity to work hard.

Yes, that kind of stereotype did exist, but—

"Mm, well," she said, "maybe that's really it in my case."

"But then…"

Maybe that really was it.

Ironically enough.

There was no other way to put it.

But then, that wasn't a bad thing.

"What are you up to, Araragi?"

Suddenly.

Hanekawa changed the subject.

Her expression had completely shifted, too—back to her normal sociable smile.

Her usual expression—which was what made it so creepy.

Think of the conversation we were in the middle of.

"It's Golden Week right now, you're not using it to study?"

"Yes, it's Golden Week… Why should I spend it studying?"

"Haha!" Hanekawa let out a cheerful laugh. "I use my holidays—to go on walks."

"……"

"I don't want to be at home. Just the thought of spending all day together with those two parents of mine—makes me shudder."

"Do you…have a bad relationship with them?"

"It's a bigger problem than that," Hanekawa said. "We don't have a relationship. Me and my parents—and my dad and my mom, too. We're a family, but we don't talk."

"Your dad and your mom, too?"

"Yeah. Maybe it's because of me, but at some point, it was like neither of them had any affection for the other. I think it'd be better if they split up, but again, society—you do have to worry about how society sees you. They're waiting until I'm an adult, is what they say. Even though they don't have any relation to me whatsoever, ha ha."

Don't laugh.

You shouldn't be talking about that kind of thing—while you laugh.

It wasn't like her.

But what would be like her?

If the normal Hanekawa was the respectable, honorable Tsubasa Hanekawa—was this Hanekawa not those things?

Either way, I realized something then.

I figured it out.

Why I'd met Hanekawa during spring break.

If she used her holidays to go on walks, it didn't mean just Golden Week. She'd walk during spring break, summer break, and more—meeting her there that day was of course a coincidence, but there was also a reason behind the coincidence.

"So that's why I use my holidays to go on walks."

"…I think you're being too considerate," I said, offering a harmless opinion.

It was the only thing I could bring myself to say.

I hated how shallow I was.

A family that didn't relate to one another wasn't a rare occurrence, either.

What was rare was that a girl like Hanekawa had grown up in that kind of family—though I was sure she'd hate that kind of tendentious view, too.

I felt like I now had a decent understanding of why Hanekawa hated being treated like a celebrity. And why she insisted on thinking of herself as an average girl whose only notable quality is being a little on the serious side. That could've been my imagination talking again, a mistaken feeling of understanding, or something like sympathy—

"………"

But.

That's when I realized all of a sudden.

The unimaginable and complicated family situation that Tsubasa Hanekawa, model student and class president among class presidents, had to deal with—I understood that. It had been a little too complicated for me to fathom at first, but I now had a clear grasp thanks to her cogent explanation. The idea that her background might have acted as the backbone of her personality, her excessively serious nature (and how she didn't want people thinking that)—I'd been persuaded of that, too. But.

But.

That didn't explain why half of her face was covered in gauze.

It didn't begin to explain that.

Wasn't that what we were supposed to be talking about?

"…Right," she said.

And again—Hanekawa looked as though she'd failed.

This time it seemed like she'd failed plain and simple.

"What am I saying…" she muttered. "I actually am just venting at you."

"I mean, it's fine with me—"

"Promise you won't tell anyone?"

She didn't have to tell me.

She'd only happened across me and didn't need to go that far—it was fine if all she'd done was vent.

But no matter who she was with, she tried to be irreproachable, to be right, to be sincere, so now she had to tell me why the gauze was on her face.

Even though there was no need.

Even though I had no right to hear it.

"I...promise."

"My dad hit me this morning," she let the words out with a smile.

A bashful, almost embarrassed smile.

That, too—was the same as ever.

I only seem to be able to notice these things in hindsight, but I think this might have been the last straw that triggered Tsubasa Hanekawa. Not that her father hit her—but her telling me about it.

That I learned about it.

If that wasn't stressful—then what was?

"He hit you? That's—"

But I didn't realize then.

I was just surprised.

No, you could go so far as to say I was scared.

A father hitting his own daughter? It seemed—impossible to me. No, I'd never even considered the possibility. I thought it was something they made up in dramas and movies. Regardless of blood relations or family situations—it was something that should never happen.

I looked at Hanekawa's face.

The concealed left side.

It wasn't an injury from too much loving, playful contact—

"That's not all right!"

She had to deal with discord and strain at home.

That in itself wasn't tragic.

Everyone carries some kind of baggage—just as you shouldn't discriminate against someone for their birth or upbringing, you shouldn't pity or envy them, either. Even if they're obvious, noticeable issues, it isn't necessarily tragic or anything—that much is true.

But not if they get hit. That wasn't all right.

Hanekawa explained why.

Why she got hit.

It didn't begin to placate me, a third party to it—but I knew quite well that you shouldn't interject yourself into someone else's family life. Whether I was placated or not, my feelings didn't have anything to do with it.

Basically, the same thing sometimes happened at school, too.

Hanekawa always wanted to be in the right, so it wasn't rare for her to clash head-on with others—she just so happened to clash with her father this time around.

And he just so happened to answer her with violence.

"I thought you said—you didn't have a relationship with anyone in your family?"

"Maybe too much so—or maybe I thought I could start one. Despite everything having balanced itself out. I guess that puts me in the wrong. I mean, just think about it, Araragi. If you were about forty—and some seventeen-year-old complete stranger starts mouthing off to you like she knows it all? You wouldn't blame yourself if you got a little upset, if you lost your temper, don't you think?"

"But still!"

A *seventeen-year-old complete stranger*?

What was that supposed to mean?

Why would she put it that way?

They may not have been related by blood, but she lived in the same house with him since she was three—weren't they family?

"You're saying you can't blame someone for getting violent? Are you sure you should be saying that? Isn't it the most unforgivable thing you—"

"Wh-Why not? It was just once."

I'd flown straight off the handle.

I didn't know why—I was probably mad at the way someone had treated Hanekawa, my personal savior. But all my anger did was chase her into a corner. She was trying to come up with some kind of compromise—while I was just brandishing the pure, unrefined truth at her.

The truth hurts.

It always does.

It was just once—she said.

If anything, I shouldn't have made her say that.

What's bad is bad, what's inexcusable is inexcusable—it was Tsubasa Hanekawa's style to be blunt about such things whether it was a friend or a teacher. So if she bluntly told one of her parents that what's bad is bad, what's inexcusable is inexcusable—then, even if she got hit for it, she'd have been able to stand tall and remain Tsubasa Hanekawa, if that were all.

And yet.

I made her say it.

Why not, it was just once—

The words—were a rejection of her whole life.

They were a rejection of her self.

"You promised, Araragi. You won't tell anyone—you promised, okay?"

Never bring it up again.

Not to the school.

Not to the police.

No, more than anyone—not to Hanekawa.

"B-But—how am I supposed to promise something like—"

"…Please, Araragi," she said. Then, maybe because she thought a promise wasn't enough—she bowed her head. "Don't tell anyone about this, please. I'll do anything if you stay quiet."

"……"

"Please."

"Yeah. Okay…"

The way she bore down on me—it was the only way I could answer.

I couldn't bring myself to press her any further. Not after being requested something as absurd as that—not after making her ask for something as absurd as that.

She'd rejected me.

And if I'd been rejected—I couldn't help her.

People went and got saved on their own, that's all—

"But at least go to the hospital. You put that gauze there yourself, didn't you? I'll admit that you're good with your hands, but even so, that looks a little on the unnatural side."

"Yeah…okay. I guess I'm not doing anything over Golden Week, anyway, so maybe I'll have a doctor look at it. I should get some use out of my insurance now and then."

"And also—if anything happens, call me. I'll come and help you, no matter where I am or what I'm doing."

"Haha," Hanekawa laughed, "where'd that come from? Look at you, sounding cool." The same smile as ever. "What do you mean by 'anything'?"

"Well, you know—"

"Yeah, I get it, Araragi."

Then she added:

"I'll call you right away if anything ever happens. Would a text be okay, too?"

That's what she said, but—

In the end, I didn't get a single call or text message from Hanekawa all Golden Week.

I said I'd be there when she needed me—however.

Hanekawa, the woman I owed my life to, never once needed me at that point—she wanted company, but only to vent, to help her feel better—she didn't need me, but I was there being useless anyway.

What she needed was a cat.

That cat.

There's a reason for an aberration.

After that, we steered clear of our earlier conversation and instead discussed our future plans for the class. We mostly talked about the culture festival. As we did, we came across a cat that had been hit by a car. It seemed to be a stray since it had no collar. A tailless white cat. We didn't know whether it was a breed born with no tail, or if its tail had been torn off during its life on the street. A white cat—it might have even seemed silver depending on how you looked at it, but the color of its fur had been ruined either way, stained with its own blood. It was in terrible shape, probably run over again and again after being hit for the first time—and Hanekawa walked out into the street from the sidewalk and picked the cat up like it was a completely natural thing to do.

"Could you help me?"

No one ever turned down such a request from Hanekawa.

We buried the cat on a nearby mountain—and that brings an end to our prologue, the first of our nine nightmarish days, April twenty-ninth.

I don't know how much of this first day, or of the conversation,

Hanekawa remembers—she was still herself so maybe she remembers burying the cat, but it's likely she forgot all of the details when she lost her memories. There's no way for me to be sure, sadly—her mind is as sharp as a steel trap, so she'd figure it out as soon as I try to check.

Now that the introduction is out of the way, the rest of the story is simple.

The next day, though I didn't have any particular business there, I was so bored that I headed to the abandoned cram school where Oshino lived, checked up on Shinobu (though her name wasn't yet Shinobu Oshino), and chatted about whatever with Oshino.

At some point, I brought up the cat we'd buried the day before.

Not because it was something else to talk about.

Because I had a bad feeling about it.

A sense of similarity—to the hell I experienced over spring break.

"Araragi. Don't tell me…" Oshino's eyes narrowed as he asked to make sure, "this was a *silver cat*?"

The chat was productive in the end.

It let us capture the aberration—an Afflicting Cat that transformed into the white-haired, white-cat-eared Black Hanekawa, named such by Mèmè Oshino—on May seventh, the last day of Golden Week, after it had spent night after night wreaking havoc in town to its heart's content.

Nine days.

It would have been dangerous had the tenth day come.

Apparently.

A speedy resolution, depending on how you looked at it—but we'd just made it in time.

With Shinobu's help (her service then was what earned her the name of Shinobu Oshino), we were able to seal away the Afflicting Cat that had bewitched Hanekawa—

Solving the problem.

With unexpected ease, you could even say.

The more complex the problem, the more likely it is to be solved with unexpected ease—because solving the problem doesn't mean it disappears.

A trance.

Hanekawa had no memories of the time she was Black Hanekawa.

That meant she didn't know the first people to be attacked by Black Hanekawa were her own parents—

Had those memories returned to her, too?

That's what I was worried about.

"Oh, the issue of her memory?"

When Black Hanekawa showed herself a week and a month since Golden Week, we managed to tie her up immediately (making use of lessons learned the last time), heard what she had to say (it barely meant a thing to us with the incessant mews, meows, nyarls, and purrs she used when she talked), and left her bound body behind in the classroom (ignoring all the curses "she" hurled at us). Then Oshino and I moved to one of the other two classrooms on the fourth floor—where the man promptly stuck an unlit cigarette in his mouth and began to speak.

We were now face to face. It was me and Oshino talking now.

"I don't think it's fatal—her memories while she's Black Hanekawa aren't compatible with her as missy class president. Her memories as miss class prez, though, could be an issue. I doubt they'll disappear this time around, because unlike last time—she's *completely* aware about her condition."

"Is it bad if she's aware of it?"

"Not that bad, in and of itself. The problem is that this is our class president we're talking about, Araragi. As you know—she's a little too wise. Her brain works about a hundred times faster than the average person's. Give her the materials and it'll be easy for her to connect all the dots and construct the memories herself."

"Construct the memories?"

"We were able to wipe out all the memories from last time. Both Black Hanekawa's and our class president's—we left her without a clue. We managed to seal that whole aberration away, which naturally meant any memories related to it disappeared, too. In other words, when we got rid of the effect, we managed to get rid of the cause, too. So it's fine if her memories are incoherent because she doesn't even realize there's anything that needs to be coherent. This time around, though, you could

145

say it'll become a fill-in-the-blank problem. Like some important words are missing here and there from a sentence—it'd be impossible to give a perfect answer, but you could figure out the general kind of words that should go in if you're perceptive enough, right?"

"Oh, so like—a language arts test."

I didn't do well in that subject.

But—Hanekawa did well in every subject.

"There's nothing we can do about it—but we ought to think of it as a silver lining that her memories from last time won't be returning. Though it'll seem more like a dark cloud to her."

We could call last time a lucky break.

But this time it was a silver lining.

"From my point of view, though, it might be a good thing for her—drawing an aberration to yourself makes it easier for aberrations to become drawn to you in the future. It's what you're experiencing right now, Araragi—so if it's going to happen to her, too, then it's important for her to know about aberrations."

You do have to be aware, Oshino said.

And—maybe he was right about that.

There are some things you can't handle without knowing about them first. While other things are unmanageable even if you do, knowing means you can at least run away from them.

In other words—that's how you maintain a balance.

"But—Oshino," I said as I thought—about Black Hanekawa, still tied up two classrooms down. "Why did—*that thing*—appear again? I thought we sealed it away during Golden Week. Wasn't it never supposed to appear again?"

"I didn't say that." Oshino tilted his head. "An Afflicting Cat, you see—is a bit different from the other aberrations you know about. If I had to compare it to any, it might be close to miss sapphy's monkey."

"Oh…I guess they are both beasts."

"Yes. Only—didn't I tell you last time? To describe it in a way that's in line with reality, the Sawarineko is a *multiple personality disorder*—Black Hanekawa is the flip side of miss class prez, so to speak. Aberrations are here, there, and everywhere—but ultimately, the Afflicting

Cat exists *only inside of our president*. It's only a trigger, a medium—the problem is the stress she bears."

Stress.

According to scholars, it is *the body's response as it tries to respond to every demand*—apparently.

"By the time Black Hanekawa faced off against me last time, she'd already gone wild for so long that you could say she'd gotten rid of most of her stress—so sealing her away was easy. But seal her away is all we did. It's not as if she disappeared. We may have made the aberration go away, but it's not as if made the stressor go away. So that thing will rise to the surface again once enough stress builds up—like a bubble."

"Stress…"

"The question is what the stressor is this time."

The cause of the stress.

In Hanekawa's case, it was of course her family.

At least, that's what I thought.

"Oh, I thought the same thing at first, too—but what do you think, Araragi? She just got rid of the stress she finally unleashed after holding herself together for seventeen years—would it really build back up to the same level in a month?"

"Well—I guess not."

"And fortunately, she hasn't been on the receiving end of any violence from either of her parents, has she?"

"No, I don't think so."

The first people she attacked.

Her dad and her mom—her parents.

Things had reverted back to normal—back to a family with no relationships that didn't communicate, a bunch of humans who just live together. That had to be stressful for Hanekawa.

But Oshino was right—one month was too soon.

Maybe if she had been hit yet again.

"We did *put a bell around her neck*—and I think that paid off," Oshino said. "It let us detect the Afflicting Cat in its early stage. See? You can never be too careful. To be honest, though, I never thought we'd actually need to use it. I was careless. I thought that even in the worst case, it would wait until she turned twenty. The story I heard made it sound like her parents were going to get divorced once she became an adult, and I'm sure her plan is to leave home by then—and that's why I didn't bother to say anything to either of you."

"Twenty, huh… So the opposite of Kanbaru."

"The age of majority is an easy measure to understand," Oshino remarked with a bitter smile. "Yes, and she'd have become strong enough to keep from being bewitched by an aberration by then."

"Oh… Anyway, Oshino. What's this bell you're talking about?"

"The headaches. She was also complaining about a headache during Golden Week, remember? So I set a little trap—though I should have shared that with you at least. So, tell me again, when did missy class president's headaches start?"

"I want to say—about a month ago?"

"Huh… And they weren't so bad at first, but then… I wonder what it could have been—but it doesn't seem like we have the time to pin down this stressor. It could very well be a mix of multiple causes, and I still understand barely a word that lust-besotted cat purrs."

"Even you don't understand her?"

Wasn't he the one saying it'd be quicker to ask her directly?

"No, I don't. We had a lot of hints, but when it comes to the exact details… It's a delicate matter, not something I can make haphazard guesses about. Heh, I guess we're dealing with a cat's brain at the end of the day. But I do also think she might just be playing dumb—we can't let our guards down, because beneath it all, she's missy class prez."

"You don't want to get on that woman's bad side."

"We haven't gotten on her bad side."

Black Hanekawa.

Another Tsubasa Hanekawa, created by her own heart and mind.

A contrasting personality—or rather, one that served as a counterpart.

In addition to aiding, "Tsubasa" also connoted pairing—mismatched wings, indeed.

"But even if we did pin down the cause, would that mean much, Oshino? Whether it's her family or something else—removing the stressor is the best way to solve this, sure, but it's not like either of us could do that."

It had been the same way last time.

Hanekawa's family problems? How could we solve something like that? I couldn't even imagine what would have to happen to her family to solve the problem. Someone on the outside couldn't step into your personal issues.

That would be true arrogance.

"And unlike the times with Senjogahara and Sengoku," I pointed out, "this aberration harms others... While it might be similar to Kanbaru's, it's different from that, too. Like before, I think our only choice is to treat the symptoms with a palliative measure—"

"Yes. You're absolutely right, but. Yeah."

Oshino was being obviously evasive.

It wasn't like him.

Did he still have something to say about the Afflicting Cat? No, it felt like he'd been acting off all day, even before I brought this up to him. Something was strange from the moment we saw him outdoors on a sunny morning—

"What's the matter, Oshino? You're being vague. Are you about to come up with some new fault you've found with me? I mean, I understand you can't help me out with this as much as you did with Sengoku, given the circumstances—"

He'd had to deal with her for a while now, and I knew Hanekawa wasn't a plain victim like Sengoku—I knew Hanekawa was relying on this aberration. Mèmè Oshino was someone who hated that.

Relying on others as long as you need them—

Then treating them like a burden once you don't.

You need to have more respect than that—he'd say.

"But aren't you obligated to help out this time around?" I pressed nonetheless. "You took her hundred thousand yen, and yet we're facing what looks like the same condition—she could practically sue you for breach of contract since you're supposed to be a professional at this. You needed to give her more aftercare. If you'd told me about that bell you said you put on her, then—"

149

"Well, I suppose you can say that."

Surprisingly enough, Oshino didn't argue with me.

It was an unthinkable reaction.

"Though I have to say, Araragi, cat ears do look good on her. Ha hah, you know what manga she reminds me of? *Neko Neko Fantasia.* You know, with the girl with the cat ears by, um, Neko Nekobe—"

"Neko Nekobe wrote *Goldfish Warning!* Don't confuse the two just because they both include the word for 'cat'... Hold on, Oshino, are you trying to gloss over something right now?"

"What do you mean, gloss over? I'd never do something that deceitful. Oh, that's right, speaking of cat ears. Arale from *Dr. Slump* used to wear them all the time too, didn't she? That manga was really ahead of its time now that I think about it. A little girl with purple hair and a weird speech tic who's also a robot and a little sister, wearing cat ears and glasses, all in one!"

"I never thought of that, but yeah, you're right... I want to tell you good analysis, but does it have anything at all to do with Hanekawa's case?"

"Ah, uh, mmm..."

He was trying to gloss over something...

He definitely was...

"Hey, Oshino. Cut it out and—"

"Kupipo!"

"Is that any way for a mature, experienced adult to gloss over whatever it is?!"

"Ehh, that's most grownups for you."

"Then I don't ever want to grow up!"

But putting aside resorting to another *Dr. Slump* reference, what exactly was he trying to distract me from?

I couldn't figure it out. And if I couldn't, there was no point in continuing to think about it. I had no choice but to keep the conversation going, even if I was half dragging it along.

"Anyway, Oshino—hurry up and bring Shinobu in. If we're up against a cat monster, our only option is to have her deal with it, right? I'm sure Shinobu is going to be reluctant, but if I offer to trade my blood for her help—"

"Hmmm. Yes, maybe. But don't you know it, disasters always strike at the worst times—misery always travels with company."

"………"

He was getting to be too evasive for me. I wished he would take this seriously. I was panicking.

This was about Hanekawa.

I wasn't needed last time, but she specifically asked for me this time around—so I had to be there for her.

I'd be there when she needed me.

"…Huh?"

And then.

That's when I remembered again—right, I'd been meaning to ask Oshino. Regarding what Hachikuji had told me about Shinobu in the morning—though I now had a sinking feeling about it.

Not that I ever had a soaring feeling about any of this!

"Hey, Oshino… There's something I wanted to ask you."

"What a coincidence. There's something I wanted you to ask me."

"What's going on with Shinobu?"

"Yep, that's the one," Oshino answered, a refreshed smile on his face, like he'd gotten something off of his chest at last, as if he were a criminal finally allowed to confess to his crimes.

"Our Shinobu has gone off on a journey of self-discovery."

0 0 7

It was night before I knew it.

I ran around town on my bike—going everywhere I could think of, but that wasn't enough. I did a second lap of the same route, literally coursing through town, but still came up almost empty-handed—before at last realizing how tired I was.

I hadn't eaten, and I hadn't drank.

I hadn't rested, just pedaling my bicycle—for nine hours.

Honestly, I was surprised. This was how much I had to do before my body got tired—and while I had fed my blood to Shinobu just the other day, most of the effects of that should have been spent healing my arms and legs—

A human mockery of a vampire.

A vampire mockery of a human.

I didn't know which I was anymore.

Shinobu Oshino.

A vampire who'd run away from home—could it get any more ridiculous? What's more, she'd disappeared with only the clothes on her back and not a penny to her name—she'd practically absconded. What kind of vampire was she?

Disasters always strike at the worst times.

Misery always travels with company.

That was exactly what had happened here.

Oshino hadn't noticed that Shinobu wasn't around until that morning—but when he thought back, he realized he hadn't seen her since the afternoon of the previous day.

According to Hachikuji's testimony, a blond girl had been sighted near the Mister Donut by the highway at five in the afternoon a day earlier—which would mean Shinobu Oshino was already busy absconding then.

She was a child. She couldn't go that far.

Only a day had passed—and Shinobu wasn't even a legendary vampire now, or anything of the sort. She was, for the most part, a simple child, one with a far weaker body than mine. A simple child—no, she'd be even weaker than that without me. The few faculties she had left would be close to cut off.

With exhaustion came hunger.

…Wait, hold on.

That was right—she could've been walking by a Mister Donut, but she didn't have a penny to her name.

Did that mean she was getting hungry?

Alone—somewhere in this town?

"………………"

While I was speeding around on my bicycle, I nearly smashed into Mayoi Hachikuji as she walked on the street—a little past noon, maybe. It was our second encounter that day. As much as I wanted to chew on my good fortune of running into Hachikuji twice in one day by chance, the only way I could meet her, there was no time. Though unlike the first time, this second meeting wasn't pure chance, strictly speaking—I was running around town with reckless abandon, so of course I'd run into her sooner or later.

"Miste rAraragi."

"Now you're just typoing my name…"

"Excuse me. Slip of the tongue."

After exchanging our greetings, I asked Hachikuji to give me a more detailed account of what she saw the day before.

"Now that you mention it," she said, "she did seem lonely, somehow."

154

"Lonely?"

"Yes," she affirmed with a serious expression. "Almost as if she were a lost child."

A lost child.

The words were particularly convincing coming from Hachikuji, a girl who'd been lost on the street for ages.

"All right," she nodded, "I'll do what I can to look for this girl too."

"Would you? I'd appreciate it."

"Yes. You see, Mister Araragi, looking for a lost child requires careful attention and manpower. Try to do it all by yourself and the hunter is sure to become the woods."

"The woods?! I'd be huge!"

"I understand you're often nonplussed, Mister Araragi, but stay strong. You can't allow yourself to get too minused."

"I know you get words wrong a lot, but you're crossing a line right now!"

"You must stay calm. When you search for a lost child, time is obsolescence."

"I agreed with you until the end there! But come on, time is of the essence!"

"I won't be able to approach her if I do find her, but I'll contact your cellular phone if I do, from a pay phone or the like."

"…Do you know how to use a pay phone?"

"Of course I do. I'm very good with mechanical devices."

"That's not what you said this morning…"

"What are you talking about? I have all the tools you need to watch television even after 2011."

"Oh, so by 'good' you mean you figured out digital broadcasting…"

"A '1seg' is something you have for breakfast, correct?"

"She's an idiot!"

All joking aside.

However good or bad she was with tech, she must be able to use a pay phone, right? I was in the one situation where I felt glad I lived in the countryside, where pay phones were still alive and kicking. Yes, this was the town I lived in, a place where every convenience store that dotted its map had a parking lot and even pachinko parlors failed to flourish.

Anyway, Hachikuji and I split up.

Just as I began to feel more positive, sure that if I met Hachikuji, I'd meet Shinobu too, I thought of something.

While I appreciated her offer to help, Hachikuji was almost the same age as Shinobu (as she appeared now). I couldn't allow myself to expect too much from her. Yes, there were some places that only children would think to search or hide in or enter into, and she could help in that respect. But while her field of activity might have been far broader than the average child's, it was still limited. She could only do so much and go so far as a child.

Meanwhile—I needed manpower.

Hachikuji was right about that, at least.

And so.

I called Sengoku's home when it was close to four. She was going to my old middle school, so I knew she'd have returned already unless she'd taken a detour on her way back. Yes, and I think she told me she was in the no-extracurriculars club—

My chances weren't all that great, but luckily she was home.

"Oh, Big Brother."

Sengoku's voice sounded lively to me. She seemed more energetic when she was talking on the phone, where you didn't have to be face to face with another person. I thought she ought to get a cell phone soon.

"You're calling me already?" she said. "I'm so happy."

"Yeah…sorry for calling you so soon. Umm…"

Uhh, where should I be starting?

Unlike when I talked to Hachikuji, I needed to explain everything from the beginning with Sengoku…

"…? What's the matter, Big Brother?"

"Oh, er…well."

"Calm down. What happened?" Sengoku asked, sounding concerned about how unclear I was being.

"Well, you see, I guess what happened is—"

"J-Just calm down for now. Calm down. O-Oh! I know. I'll tell you

156

a funny story."

"………"

I couldn't believe she said that.

How much confidence did it take to say to someone that the story you're about to tell is funny?

"While maids might be shown as living fun and carefree lives in manga and anime, being a maid is a surprisingly difficult job, you see."

"So you're the Bearcat Lover!"

No wonder the story was so hard to understand!

There's no way she'd ever been to a mixer, either!

She'd taken on a different persona in her listener's letter!

"D-Did that calm you down?"

"Yeah… I actually looped back around to being calm."

Not that I wasn't calm from the beginning.

You couldn't blame me for being careful about what I said, though.

"So," she ushered, "you wanted to tell me something?"

"Yeah… Sengoku, I wanted to ask you a favor."

"A favor… What is it?"

"I want you to find Shinobu," I said rather directly. "You're one of the few people who've seen her with your own eyes—so to be frank, you could really help by pitching in."

"Find her? Does that mean…she, er…Shinobu disappeared?"

"Yeah."

"Are you sure…she's not out on errands?"

"She never came home last night."

"O-Oh, is that so…"

From across the receiver—

I thought I could feel her hesitate.

That was right, I'd carelessly forgotten. Shinobu had glared at her persistently, according to Sengoku—she was scared of Shinobu on an instinctual level.

I made up my mind.

Sengoku shouldn't have anything to do with aberrations again, no matter how indirectly—hadn't that already been my decision? Regardless of the circumstances, what was I doing pulling her into this…

157

"Sorry, Sengoku. I should be taking care of this myself—"

"N-No. It's not like that."

"It's not like what?"

"I just thought it might sound like a lie if I answered you immediately... Let me help. Please."

"Oh... Are you sure about that, though?"

"Yeah," Sengoku said with conviction—for a change.

Could it really be because we were on the phone?

Because we weren't face to face?

"If I can pay you back that way—then I'll do it. You're searching for Shinobu—just like you helped me, right?"

"...Well, yeah."

"Then how could I not help you?"

So she was going to put it that way for me.

How could she not help me.

"I don't think anything wild is going to happen," I assured, "but I can't guarantee your safety no matter what. She might have lost most of her power, but she is a vampire..."

"It's okay." Sengoku, that reserved girl, said it with true conviction. "It's fine. Let me do it."

Now I was almost starting to feel awkward despite being the one to ask her in the first place—but Sengoku left to search for Shinobu moments later.

I felt like breathing a sigh of relief. I found myself quite glad to have the help of someone who'd met Shinobu—but I wasn't ready to breathe that sigh yet.

Sengoku couldn't ride a bike.

Well, she didn't even have one.

That was why Sengoku never touched a bicycle in traveling to that abandoned shrine the other day. She'd be searching on foot, making her only as mobile and dependable as Hachikuji.

Mobility, huh...

Yeah. Mobility.

I felt bad about asking her time and time again, case after case, but I had to now if I wanted to save Hanekawa. To begin with, there were only six people who'd seen Shinobu in her current form, and that included me—as for two more of the six, Tsubasa Hanekawa was tied up as Black Hanekawa, while Mèmè Oshino was busy standing guard over her.

That left four. Subtract me and Sengoku, and you had two.

I decided to start with the easier one to deal with, Suruga Kanbaru.

I selected her name on my phone's contact list. Her cell should have been on by now, with school already over—or maybe not. She'd only gotten one a few days earlier, so it was hard to say how familiar she was with the precise wording of the school rules, yet—

"Suruga Kanbaru here."

As always, she answered the phone with her full name.

I'd gotten myself worked up over nothing.

"Suruga Kanbaru. My special move is holding B to dash."

"......"

So that's how she saw it.

Not *takkyudo* or a flash step.

Well, I couldn't exactly call her a liar over that.

"Suruga Kanbaru. Employed as my senior Araragi's perverted slave."

"I'm absolutely going to call you a liar over that!"

"Hm? Judging by that voice and that retort, I'd say I'm talking to you."

"Did you really say *that* without even knowing you were talking to me?!"

"Oh, did the perverted slave part displease you? Well, I do understand. I was thinking of a different, more appropriate title for myself, but I decided to self-censor because it was a little too extreme."

"If *you* found it too extreme, I shudder to imagine it!"

And.

Hurry up and learn how to use a contacts list already.

"Are you at school right now, Kanbaru?"

"No, I already left."

"What? Really? What about preparing for the culture festival?"

"It wasn't my turn today."

"Oh. So your class takes turns... I'm jealous, you guys sound pretty

159

well-organized."

Right.

Her phone wouldn't have been on if she was at school.

"Uh, so does that mean you're at home right now, Kanbaru?"

"No, not that either. It's not like you to guess wrong twice in a row, is something the matter? So it's true, even the mightiest can fall. Right now I'm amusing myself by playing *Fashionable Witches: Love and Berry* in the neighborhood supermarket's game room."

"How was I supposed to predict that?!"

Damn it, she was always undermining my expectations!

Couldn't she ever act like I thought she might for a change?

"Um, I'm not super familiar with that game, but is that actually fun for high schoolers to play?"

"What are you talking about? Great games can be enjoyed by people of any age. I've already spent nearly three thousand yen today alone. There's a small line of kids behind me, but I don't have any intention of giving up my seat."

"You're acting like a terrible person just because you have some money! What are you doing?! Stop right now and let those kids play!"

"Hmph. My senior, of all people, saying the same thing as that clerk who just kicked me out of the store."

"You got kicked out?!"

"If someone gets angry at you for real, the only thing to do is get just as angry back at them."

"No! You need to apologize for real!"

"Even if I'm being told the same thing, an order from you is different. Fine, I'll go to the next machine down and start playing *Mushiking*…"

"Stop playing those!"

"It's important to always stay playful. It's through play, not study, that we've grown and etched our history as humans. Oh, that's right. Speaking of which, a little while back, I was playing cards with two friends and we decided to play President…"

"So you're 'Oracle's Auricle'?!"

I couldn't believe the girl.

She was so cute.

So cute that she never became too cute for me.

"All right then, my senior Araragi. Why don't you tell me why you called?"

"Right…"

I couldn't talk to her about anything serious without some stupid banter first, so I'd write our conversation so far off as a necessary introduction.

"Kanbaru. I want you to lend me your strength."

"Lend it to you? Don't be silly. My strength belongs to you from the start. All you have to do is tell me how to use it."

"……"

That was actually cool…

It was a cool, grown-up thing to say.

Even though she was amusing herself by playing video games meant for children…

I began to wonder. Why did she have such a hardboiled personality? That, at least, couldn't have been Senjogahara's influence…

"I want you to find Shinobu. That twerp ran away from home."

"She ran away from home?"

"She absconded, in other words."

"Oh. Okay, then. That's all I need to hear. So you're saying I need to strip?"

"If you're that desperate to, then you're welcome to take off all the clothes you want next time we're alone! We can both do it, we'll make a contest out of taking it all off and showing it all off! Heh, you're going to be blown away if you ever see me strip! So please, Kanbaru, hold off on that for now and just find Shinobu like a normal person would find someone! I hate to say it, but I'm putting more hope in you than anyone else! I need you to lend me those legs that can run faster than a bike!"

"Lend them to you? Don't be silly. My calves, thighs, knee pits, shins, ankles, and groin all belong to you from the start."

"That doesn't sound very hardboiled to me!"

"What was that? The soles of my feet? Now there's the man I've come to know. So kinky that you fear no gods…"

161

"I never said that!"

She was a total pervert!

She just ruined all of Senjogahara's careful spin!

"You're overestimating me. I'm not that much of a pervert," denied Kanbaru. "The words 'women-only train car' gets me terribly excited, but that's where it stops."

"That already makes you unique!"

"Ah, so you acknowledge me as your perverted slave at the end of the day."

"No, I never called you my slave!"

"I just remembered. Speaking of kinky acts."

"That's how you keep this conversation going? You do realize we're still in high school…"

"Fine, then we can say indecent acts instead. I understand that you engaged in an indecent act with her last night."

"………"

Why did Kanbaru know?

Well, actually, if she knew, that meant…

"That's right, I heard it straight from her. She said she engaged in an indecent act with you under the stars."

"There's nothing indecent about a kiss, is there?!"

Maybe you could extrapolate from there, but did I not want to see it that way because I was a little boy?

"And wait, Senjogahara goes around talking about stuff like that?"

What an open person…

There was nothing about it to feel guilty over, we were boyfriend and girlfriend…but it did feel like she could afford to be more tactful.

"Did she tell you today at school?"

"No, I heard about it last night. Well, I say I heard about it, but… it's more like she forced the information on me, calling me in the dead of the night and bragging about it for five hours or so."

"What an annoying senior!"

That meant Senjogahara had been up nearly all night, even if she'd called right after getting back from the observatory. She didn't show any signs of being sleepy when I met her in the morning, though… Did she wear an iron mask or something? You can only be so expressionless.

Still, Senjogahara was bragging? So it was something to brag about. Hitagi Senjogahara never struck me as the type to talk herself up, but then again, not only were she and Kanbaru junior and senior, they were both girls.

So she'd talk, huh?

That was a little surprising to learn.

"Allow me to congratulate you," Kanbaru said.

"Oh… Thanks."

"But I don't want you thinking that you've won quite yet."

"Was that a declaration of war?!"

"Love means never having to say sorry…to you!"

"Hold on, to me?!"

We were getting way too off track.

Even so, she was mobile enough to make up for all my wasted time and more…

The strong always have a fundamental advantage.

They get to do what they want.

"In any case, yes," Kanbaru reiterated. "You're saying you just want me to find that cute blond girl. I hear you loud and clear. If it's a request coming from you, then I'm really going to run. Heheheh, however big the world is, only three things out there can get me sprinting for real: my two dear seniors and BL novel release dates."

"At the risk of being misunderstood, I'm going to say it doesn't make me particularly happy to be on that list!"

Actually, no. I didn't want to be on it at all.

She needed to make that last one a separate category.

"You know," she footnoted, "even though I go for most any boys' love genre, there are a few that I still can't get into… Some of those novels wouldn't make me sprint for real."

"Enough!"

And.

They might not get her serious, but it sounded like she bought them anyway.

"But didn't you take your basketball matches seriously before you retired?" I asked her.

"If I have to give an answer, then I'd say no, contrary to expectations. I'd tear up the floor in the gym if I got serious."

"Sorry, is your body a tank or something?!"

"And, well, you leave behind afterimages if you move around too fast in a small area like that. Basketball is played with five people a team, so cloning techniques are against the rules."

"Don't mess with the level of realism of our world for no good reason! Aberrations are enough, people can't actually leave behind afterimages!"

"Being called for traveling would be a more pressing issue than the number of players."

"Refs shouldn't be calling beginner fouls like traveling if a player's cloning herself, should they!"

"I can get up to nine people by cloning myself. If I can just make one more, I'd be able to visualize an entire match on my own."

"No, you wouldn't! That's not possible, of course it's not! You won't fool me no matter how detailed your explanation gets!"

"A request from you is a different story, though. I think I'll try taking off my limiters for once and running like I mean it."

"I don't know, part of me feels like it wants to stop you?!"

I wasn't sure if she was kidding.

She was as dangerous as a junior could get. A ballistic missile.

"There's no point in trying to stop me. I've received an order from my senior, and nothing could make me happier. I'll vow to you right now, I'm going to run until I can't move another step."

"Listen, you don't need to push yourself. I know you're fast, but didn't you tell me before that you weren't good at running long distances or something?"

"Huh? Oh, don't worry, that was part of my character and background story when I first appeared, before I really started to take shape."

"Don't say that kind of thing out loud!"

"If it really bothers you that much, then I wouldn't mind reverting back to those defaults."

"Stop talking like you're a video game options menu!"

Well.

When Kanbaru said she wasn't good at running, it was different from when I said it. I didn't have too much to worry about.

"Heheheh. Now that I've received an order from you, my old name won't do. Having evolved, I should assume a new one. That's right, I'm no longer Suruga Kanbaru—I'm Omega Kanbaru."

"Be still my heart!"

"Incidentally, if a marina evolves, it becomes a mariner."

"Sounds both tougher and fouler!"

"And if a 'Caution: Falling Rocks' sign evolves, it becomes a 'Caution: Falling Meteors' sign."

"Hold on, I don't need that much evolution!"

What would happen if I evolved?

I actually wanted to give that a little thought.

"Anyway, Kanbaru. If you find Shinobu—um, I actually don't know about you. There is the stuff with your left arm, so I wonder if you'd be okay... No, you'd still be in danger if that's all you had. Okay, so if you find Shinobu, do not approach her, just contact me immediately."

"What? You're saying I can't run up and hug her?!"

"No!!"

In more ways than one, because none of them would turn out well.

"Hold on there," complained Kanbaru. "I can't have you making light of me like that. My life isn't so dear to me that I wouldn't trade it in to cuddle with a little girl."

"Well, it's going to have to be dear to you for now... And what's so great about getting to cuddle with a little girl, anyway?"

"How could you need anything more to be happy in life?!"

"You're mad at me!"

My own junior, mad at me! Over not knowing I only needed a cute little girl to be happy in life!

"Putting your principles and beliefs aside, Kanbaru... I think I'm the only person in the world right now who could stand up to Shinobu, realistically speaking—Oshino can't for his own reasons. Okay?"

"Okay."

"Sengoku is helping out too, so fill each other in if you happen to meet... Oh, right. Sengoku gave me your volleyball shorts and school swimsuit to hold onto."

"Oh, thank you. They're not washed, are they?"

"Uh, I think they are."

"Excuse me?!"

She'd shouted. She really needed to do something about her characterization...

"Foolish..." she muttered. "It was all meaningless if they're washed... It's unlike you to allow such a travesty."

"Um, how exactly do you see me? Do you expect me to stop a middle schooler from washing a pair of volleyball shorts and a school swimsuit that she wore?"

"I can't believe you... How could you be this cruel? You gave me hope, only to snatch it away seconds later... I'd surely have committed suicide by now if I had potassium cyanide with me here..."

"The premise that you'd ever have any with you is far-fetched in the first place..."

So it was something she'd want to kill herself over?

Is that how she saw herself?

"My senior Araragi, I truly regret having to say this to you of all people, but I have no choice. It looks like you're going to have to pay for this blunder."

"........."

Why, exactly?

At the same time, I couldn't let this put a dent in Kanbaru's motivation...

The strong really do enjoy certain perks...

"Understand?" she asked.

"Yeah, yeah...just tell me what I need to do."

"You only need to 'aah' once."

"Is that supposed to be romantic?!"

What was even going on now?

"I just said that I'll make it up to you. I'd be happy to pay you recompense. What do you need me to do?"

"Okay, then. You need to sleep in those volleyball shorts and school swimsuit for a night, sweat like crazy into them, and return them to me unwashed. If you do that, I'll forgive you."

"You realize that actually doing that would make us both perverts of the highest order?! Actually, it might leave you even worse off than me!"

"Sounds like a fun path to walk down, so long as you're by my side."

"I'm sorry, Kanbaru, but I'm not ready to die with you!"

"Then I could always force our lovers' suicide."

"That's called a murder-suicide!"

"We better think of how to go about this some other time."

"No, think better of it right now!"

"Anyway, you said Sengoku's helping us out too? In that case, it feels like—there are a handful of people on this."

"Yeah. I know this might not sound very convincing after all the time we've wasted talking nonsense—but every second counts. Please, Kanbaru. Help us."

"Of course. I'm so on board that it brings tears to my eyes. It's not in me to say no to you. I act only according to your orders," Kanbaru said, then hung up.

She was supposedly at the neighborhood supermarket, but neighborhood or not, there was only one supermarket in the area… You could call it our podunk town's one lifeline, so I began to feel honestly worried that Kanbaru was now holding B and tearing up the flooring as she dashed outside—but it was heartening to have her on board, that nonsensical and unrealistic concern aside.

So. On to the last person.

The last person with first-hand knowledge of Shinobu—

I called Hitagi Senjogahara's number.

The phone rang for an awfully long time—it felt like I waited almost twenty seconds. Right as I was wondering if I was going to be sent to voice mail, the call went through at last.

"I'm not going."

"………"

She opened with a refusal.

What was she, psychic?

167

And she'd said no, too...

"It felt like it took you forever to pick up the phone, did something happen?"

"No? Not particularly? It was too much of a bother to pick up the phone, and I let it sit in my pocket without checking who the caller was, but it rang for so long that I gave up and checked only to see that it was you, which made me think I didn't have to pick up after all, so I went to press the power button to hang up on you but accidentally pressed the call button instead and had no choice but to take it. What do you want?"

"Why would I want anything from you now?!"

What a horrible person.

She never showed any signs of letting up, even on the phone.

"Anyway, Senjogahara—could you hear me out?"

"No. In fact, you're the one who needs to hear me out. So I went to a video rental store the other day with my friend."

"So you're 'Ain't Nothin' Like a Found Dog'?! You haven't had a single friend for years! Now that I know you pretended to have one to write in to a radio station, what was meant to be a funny letter just sounds sad to me!"

And what kind of ratings was this radio show getting?

Was everyone listening to it?!

Everyone except me?!

Popular culture had left me behind!

"Please, Senjogahara. Forget about that and listen to me."

"I guess I have no choice if you're getting down on all fours."

"I'm not!"

"So, what is it?"

"...Shinobu disappeared."

"Shinobu—that blond kid?"

"Yeah."

"Hmph."

No thoughts.

Indifferent and insensitive.

Of course, while she may have been acquainted with Shinobu, it wasn't as if she'd ever spoken or socialized in any way with her—and not just Senjogahara. Kanbaru and Sengoku, too. Of us all, the only people who knew what Shinobu was like on the inside were me, Oshino, and—Hanekawa.

"You went so far as to play hooky to find this girl?"

"Yeah. Which is why I want you to help out. The only people who've met Shinobu in person—"

"But," Senjogahara interrupted me, "that couldn't have been what you meant by 'humanitarian aid' this morning—you'd never refer to that kid as human."

"......"

"Hanekawa took today off from school," Senjogahara added impassively.

She didn't betray any emotion. I could practically see her ever-expressionless face. Had this girl really called Kanbaru to brag all night about what she'd done?

"Could it be related in any way? Oh, you don't have to answer that. Your silence is eloquent," she said.

"Even if it is, I'm going to answer you. Yes, you're exactly right. Hanekawa's—"

"Now that you mention it, Mister Oshino did say something about that—the girl did good work during Hanekawa's case, or something. Is that what this is? You need that girl's abilities for Hanekawa's sake, but she's absconded for other reasons?"

"You have really good intuition, you know that? And a good memory, too."

"I'm confident about my memory. I even remember when the Kamakura Shogunate was founded."

"Only the most generic Japanese history question ever..."

"In eleven hundred ninety-two, they formed that useless *bakufu*."

"What a mean mnemonic!"

"You know, Araragi, you sound equally worried about the two, Hanekawa and the kid—impartial in your concern, even though it's obvious whom you ought to be prioritizing. That's so like you."

"......?"

169

What was she saying?

I was supposed to be prioritizing?

What did that have to do with the situation we were in?

It wasn't like what happened with Sengoku. We weren't in a position where we had to choose who to save—were we?

"I'm not going," Senjogahara repeated. "I won't be going anywhere."

"Hey, Senjogahara—"

"I need to prepare for the culture festival, after all."

"Well, okay…I understand that, but right now we're—"

"Hanekawa entrusted me with this."

Those were powerful words.

Powerful and willful—like a drawn sword.

"How could I possibly sneak away? And the more danger Hanekawa is in, the more I'm needed here to fulfill my role."

She was right—

It was no ordinary case of being asked to help.

Hanekawa had entrusted Senjogahara with those duties under pressure from an aberration. How could Senjogahara skip out on that to look for Shinobu?

"Not to mince words, the chain of command is in chaos without Hanekawa here—nothing is working right. She was dealing with all of this? She has to be insane to put together this schedule. And you're not here, either, the one person who was supporting her—honestly, I can't even afford to be wasting time on the phone like this."

"Well, Hanekawa was doing most of it by herself—"

Just how much of herself had she devoted to our class? And—just how hard had she worked to keep them from noticing? Did she never show them any of the toil she was going through? She could have easily been swamped with all the work she had, yet she never showed any sign of being busy—not a single complaint escaped her lips. It was that way with everything she did—what was impressive wasn't how hard she worked, but how she never allowed anyone to catch on. I was right by her, supporting her all this time, and even I had a hard time saying I fully grasped everything she was going through.

Honestly.

She, and no one else, really was the real deal—

......

Though I did wish Miss Hitagi wouldn't dismiss speaking to her boyfriend on the phone as a waste of time…

"I doubt I'll be able to go home until pretty late," she said, "and it looks like there's no way I'd be able to finish by the time school closes. I'll probably have to take this home with me and work on it there. I'm almost astonished she was doing this much during school hours. Listen, Araragi. You just need to do what you always do—and I'll do what I always do."

"Yeah… All right, then," I relented, having understood the situation very well. "You take care of school. Let's make this a good culture festival."

"Yes. I'd like that."

The same flat tone as ever.

She seriously didn't betray a single emotion.

That was still what Senjogahara said, though.

"Okay—I'll call you again later," I told her.

"Oh, Araragi. Just one more thing?"

"What is it?"

"Your tsundere bonus," she wrapped up. In her flat tone. "Don't misunderstand, it's not like I'm worried about you or anything—but I'll never forgive you if you don't come back, okay?"

She cut the call off there.

She nearly took my consciousness with her, but I somehow managed to endure.

Oh, god… I really didn't know what to say. Every single time I talked to her, she… No, I don't mind being told my vocabulary is lacking… I just don't have any other words for it.

I loved her so much.

So much I didn't know what to do.

Of course I'd come back.

If she was waiting for me, of course I would.

"…Don't worry, you can count on me."

In any case.

I had now asked everyone I could for their help.

It was the extent of my third-year high school network.

It may have only been a consolation, in perspective—the situation may not have shifted by much, but still—

My confidence was on another level.

I pedaled and pedaled and pedaled and pedaled and pedaled and pedaled—then continued for another three hours.

I had now been searching for nine hours.

Seven p.m.

Before I knew it—it was night.

I hadn't eaten, and I hadn't drank.

I hadn't rested—

And I was finally feeling tired.

"Still...what is Shinobu thinking?"

Running away from home—really?

Absconding—really?

A journey of self-discovery—really?

When you shouldn't be able to go anywhere—

Just like me.

"..............."

It all started—during spring break.

It all started with my second-year closing ceremony.

It was a while ago by now.

I learned of the existence of aberrations—

I became an aberration myself—

And it's been that way ever since.

A demon.

A cat.

A crab.

A snail.

A monkey.

A snake.

And then, once again...a cat.

A Changing Cat—an Afflicting Cat.

Black Hanekawa—another Tsubasa Hanekawa.

In most cases, cat monsters turned into humans—countless legends all went the same way. It first eats an old lady, changes into that old lady, enters her house, then eats everyone else.

A cat changes into a human.

And then—eats them.

But an Afflicting Cat did the opposite—no, perhaps you could call it an interpretation of the same legends from a different angle. *Cases where a cat doesn't change into a human—but where a human changes into a cat.* Cat monsters who turn into humans are spotted because of their odd behavior—but with Afflicting Cats, that unnatural behavior is understood as a case of multiple personalities. If you focused on only that element, it was similar to cases of foxes possessing humans. There's a way that most folk tales about Afflicting Cats go—night after night, a virtuous wife turns into a harlot and walks the streets—then a traveling monk (or maybe a warrior, or maybe a hunter) declares that it's the work of a cat monster and takes action—*only to discover it was just the wife all along.*

If you were to take only the ending of the stories into consideration, then yes, at no point does a cat ever appear in the tale. The reader is given a little peek at a white cat with no tail, but it's nothing more than a plot conceit, or something used to make the story more engaging—but the theme, the anchor, is humanity itself.

The obverse and reverse sides of humans.

Hanekawa in reverse—the black, awful Tsubasa Hanekawa.

No—should that be white?

Either way, there was no arguing she'd been consumed, but—

I wanted to hear what Kanbaru had to say.

The Afflicting Cat and Kanbaru's monkey did seem similar—though they were probably only similar and not the same. The biggest difference was that all the monkey had done was grant Suruga Kanbaru's wishes according to a fair and reasonable contract—while the Afflicting Cat was on Tsubasa Hanekawa's side, thoroughly and through and through, unconditionally and without reserve. During Golden Week, it attacked me, Oshino, and even Hanekawa herself in the end, with both malice and hostility—but even that was for Hanekawa's sake. It may not have been what she wanted or wished for—but the cat was on her side.

It wasn't just on her side—it was *her*, after all.

That was the difference with Kanbaru's monkey.

Kanbaru. She'd still be running around.

But—she hadn't called.

No one had called.

We hadn't just failed to find our first hint, we were clueless.

What did it mean?

A blond girl would be the most conspicuous person in the entire town—yet we didn't even have an eyewitness?

Could she have already skipped town somehow?

No, her legs were a child's…at least, they should have been.

She shouldn't be able to do anything—without me at her side.

I looked up at the sky.

Night.

No trace left of dusk.

There were stars in the sky—it was nothing like the one I'd seen the night before by the observatory… Even so, the stars were pretty. I had a feeling I'd be making a habit out of looking up at the sky—since it was a memory that I shared with Senjogahara.

Everything.

So she said.

That's about everything I can give you—

But no, she was wrong.

Just look. She'd given me these memories.

Not only of that starry sky—of it all, from our first contact on the stairs to the present moment.

Memories… And memory.

Hanekawa's memory—would never be wiped again. Personally, I thought losing all memory of ever getting involved with an aberration might be for the best—but perhaps Oshino was right in the end.

Not just in the way he meant.

Me, too—I didn't want to forget, either.

That spring break.

That hell.

174

It all started from there, after all—

"…Shinobu—Shinobu Oshino."

I'd find her, no matter what.

I'd find her, and I'd show her.

I decided to be responsible for you for the rest of my life—

"Okay… That's enough of a break."

I started pedaling again. I'd recovered most of my stamina from the breather—I really did have an absurd body.

The stars in the sky aside—it was getting to be late.

A little longer and I'd need Sengoku, a middle schooler, to go back home. We were already short-handed, and that would cut down on our forces. Filing a police report about a missing child was out of the question, given the circumstances…

The night part was a little concerning, too.

It goes without saying that vampires—are nightwalkers. You couldn't call Shinobu a vampire any longer, but it was true that her activities were less limited at night. As it deepened, so did her powers.

And so did the danger.

It was past seven now… The next two hours were crucial.

I need to hurry, I thought, standing up from my bike's saddle and pedaling as hard as I could—until, with a thunk, both of my pedals grew heavy and my speed dropped like a car whose emergency brake had been pulled.

I thought I'd broken my bike at first after going too hard on it. Either my chain had snapped or my tires had blown…but that wasn't the case.

Someone had jumped onto my back seat.

No, "someone" might not be the right word.

If I had to say, it was a cat.

"……"

"Meow."

"……"

Right…

Just like vampires…cats were nocturnal, too.

White hair, cat ears, still in her pajamas—

A woman I knew well.

She'd taken her glasses off—she saw well in the dark.

The look she was giving me, though, was awful... And it wasn't just her eyes. Her entire expression was so sour that I couldn't believe she could make it with her face.

She'd taken off her long-sleeved blouse—she must have felt hot.

So, "The North Wind and the Sun" was right after all. I finally happened to get a glance at Hanekawa in her pajamas from head to toe, but I'd have been twice as happy had she not been in her present state.

And so.

Black Hanekawa was there.

"...Why are you here?"

"Rolly-meow."

"Answer me."

I didn't want to hear some fake cat sound in reply.

We'd placed Black Hanekawa under tight bonds in that abandoned cram school, under Oshino's tight watch. So why—

"Don't be such a sourpuss, human. Rolly-rolly."

"And I'm not going to let you pussyfoot around my question."

"Hmph. No purrticular reason. So stop giving me that dubious look, human. Not sure why, but I clawed myself out of those ropes like it was nyothing when I was pawing around just a minute ago."

"Just a minute ago..."

Oh—right.

She was nocturnal.

Even during Golden Week, it was always around noon when a small bit of Hanekawa as Hanekawa managed to resurface—this aberration's power and control was overwhelmingly stronger at night. Hmm, that was another thing it had in common with Kanbaru's monkey.

"Myaa-hahaha!" Black Hanekawa laughed in delight.

It probably didn't mean anything.

She was laughing for no reason.

She had the intelligence of a cat, too—Oshino had said something about her being missy class president underneath, but it didn't seem that way to me... In her current state, Tsubasa Hanekawa didn't seem

176

to have any reverse side.

Actually, no.

This already was Hanekawa in reverse.

If she had any, it'd be her obverse side.

"But what about Oshino standing guard?"

"I'm a cat. Mewving around without making a sound is kitty's play to me."

"Now that you mention it…I guess you're right."

Oshino was proving to be incredibly useless this time around.

It wasn't like him.

His odd demeanor when we first arrived at the abandoned cram school and the evasiveness he'd shown thereafter could be attributed to Shinobu's disappearance (he must have been outside looking for her), but letting Black Hanekawa escape so easily? It seemed unthinkable.

It was right after Shinobu had run away.

He wasn't the kind of man to make the same stupid mistake twice in a row.

Wait, don't tell me he'd done it on purpose… Had he freed Black Hanekawa? Did he tie her up in knots that were only strong enough to keep her there during the day (the Afflicting Cat's words, "clawed myself out of them like it was nothing," supported the idea) and pretend not to notice as she got away?

She must have pinned down my location simply through her sense of smell and hearing.

That was how cats hunted.

The question, though, was why she'd come to me after being freed— the reason, not the method. If Oshino had intentionally allowed her to escape, that of course made this yet another instance of things conforming to his know-it-all stance…

But if so, why?

Another reason that eluded me.

One thing I did know was that he'd used a "heterodox" method, or whatever he wanted to call it, to summon the Afflicting Cat by force because he "didn't have time"—because he wanted to talk to it directly. He claimed that she made just as little sense to him as she did to me, but he was a master of self-effacement. Could he have found a hint in her incoherent babble, or at least a trace of one?

"Hey, cat…"

"Myes?"

"……"

I got off my bike, held its handlebars with one hand, and turned to face Black Hanekawa who sat on my back seat, only to involuntarily swallow the words I was about to rain down on her.

I was left speechless.

Wow… I could see every curve in her body now that she'd taken off that blouse. I'm talking up the fact that she was in pajamas, but come to think of it, they were just pajamas. Even so, she was impossibly hot. Forget what I said earlier about potentially being twice as happy. I mean, the slightest movement and her breasts were bouncing everywhere. Boingy. Boingy. That onomatopoeia isn't a sound a human body should ever make. Forget about moving the story forward, forget about narrative coherence, I wanted to throw it all out and spend all night jumping rope with her.

Kanbaru might talk dirty, but Hanekawa's body…

Plus she had cat ears.

It scared me just to imagine her with black hair.

I understood that physical sex appeal was an absolute necessity for continuing the species, but was there any need to go this far?

"What's the myatter?"

"A, er—um."

Then again, she went on her Golden Week rampage in her underwear… This was way easier in comparison. No matter how much of Hanekawa's memory returned, that one needed to stay erased from her brain for eternity.

"…Um, okay, cat. Repeat after me. 'Now, the manic maniac mused, mentally mangling mammalian mammaries naturally atrophied.'"

"Meow, the myanic myaniyac mewsed, meowntally myangling myameowlian meowmyaries nyaturally meowtrophied."

"So! Damn! Cute!!"

I'd managed to use my love of cat talk to find a replacement for

178

jumping rope.

A brilliant call, if I do say so myself.

Wait, no.

"I was going to ask you what you're here for."

"That must be your way of meowing hello," she said mockingly. "To purrsent ya with my help, human. Why else would I have come?"

"To—help me?"

"Don't be mistaken, human—I'm nyot interested in fighting ya any longer. Didn't I tell ya that a mewnute ago?"

"A minute ago…"

Oh…she meant this morning.

Who calls half a day earlier "a minute ago"? That's an aberration for you, their grasp on time is just… No, maybe it was best to think of it here as a cat's intellect being unable to grasp the concept of time.

Plus.

"Did you ever…tell me that?"

"Oh, myaybe not. It doesn't myatter anyway, because I just did. I don't intend to go on any rampage this time—I'm not in that kind of mewd today."

"…………"

Could I…believe her?

There was no way I could if I took last time into consideration… But on the other hand, that was the normal way to look at it. Trying to read too much into what this cat said left you looking like a fool.

If she said it wasn't her intention—then maybe it wasn't.

And—

If she said she was here to help, then she really was here to help.

"But—why? You're like…Hanekawa's stress, right? A second personality she has that manifested to reduce her stress—"

That—was how the nightmare started.

She attacked her parents, she attacked innocent bystanders in town—she went on an unfettered rampage. She was utterly audacious about it, too. It wasn't quite as bad as the hell that was my spring break in terms of damage—but the Afflicting Cat may have surpassed even the vampire in terms of dread. She indiscriminately attacked people with all the drive of an adolescent boy who hid at school until night in order to smash all its windows, unable to hold it in any longer—it was a preposterous stress relief method.

"So don't get the wrong idea—I still feel like thanking ya. Nyormally it would've taken a year to relieve my meowster's stress, but it only took nine days thanks to you—"

Oh…

So you could look at it that way, too.

Of course, from the Afflicting Cat's point of view—all she cared about was venting Hanekawa's stress. So no matter how simple, hasty, or *efficient* the method—it didn't matter.

To the very end, aberrations—were logical.

"Ah…so you want to find Shinobu as soon as possible, too. You're saying—our interests align."

"Purr-cisely."

"…Okay," I nodded.

I still had my doubts, but there was no time to hesitate.

"In that case, your help is exactly what I need."

"Myaa-haha. So you could say that my offer to ya…is the cat's pajamas!!"

"………!"

The Hanekawa I knew would never look so triumphant over that obvious and stupid of a joke…

But this was Hanekawa's flipped personality.

It was kind of depressing.

"Well, I'm more interested in your feline senses of smell and hearing. You've fought her before, so you ought to know her scent and her voice. All you need to do is track those."

"Hmm. All righty."

"I'm going to ride around at random, so let me know if you notice something, okay?"

I got back on my bike.

With Black Hanekawa on its back seat.

It might be a lie to say that I didn't have a single wicked thought in my mind at that moment. Okay, it would be a lie. That plump sensation from when I rode with Hanekawa that morning was still fresh in my mind. But my vulgar motives were met with instant karma of the highest order.

"Gah!"

I reflexively fell from my bike, and the momentum caused it to crash to the ground as well. Only one person, no, cat survived, Black Hanekawa, who dexterously sprang into the air, spun, and made a clean landing.

That's a cat for you. This was no time to be impressed, though.

"Hm? What's the myatter, human?"

"…Ah, gaah…ah—"

The Afflicting Cat afflicted in more ways than one.

To give a modern name to a particularly notable characteristic of this type of cat monster, they were able to drain one's energy. In this way, she was less like a cat monster and more like a succubus, incubus, or *jurei*. She was a lust-besotted cat. *An aberration that consumed humans— those she touched found their strength and vitality sucked dry.* There was no case of it being bad enough to kill someone—but at the very least, she did send some people to the hospital over Golden Week.

She sent two people to the hospital.

Hanekawa's parents.

Of course—they were discharged in three days or so.

This was the aberration that had fully embraced me as she sat on my back seat… It was only for a moment, and while you could write off whatever small bit of resistance there was, unlike during Golden Week, Black Hanekawa was now wearing proper clothes, pajamas though they may be—so I wasn't sucked dry in an instant, but I was wearing light clothing myself…which meant I took an incredible amount of damage. Just as I thought I had recovered my stamina, it disappeared again in a flash.

Energy drain.

Still, allow me to say this.

I may have fallen, but I had no regrets!

"……………"

I started to think that I might really be misunderstood if I kept saying those kinds of things… It wasn't that I was trying to be considerate of anyone in particular, but Senjogahara did have an awfully good sense for it…

You can never be too careful.

"Oh, I get it, human. My myaster's breasts felt so wonderful you're writhing with pleasure!"

"I'll admit that I'm stupid, but you know, you're pretty stupid, too…"

Did she not understand her own abilities?

The Afflicting Cat's ability to drain energy was always-on, activating whenever direct contact was made. It had nothing to do with the cat's intentions…

"Well, human, if you're that despurrate for it, I'll let ya myassage these breasts if we can agree to some conditions."

"Stop trying to sell your master's chastity, you lustful cat."

"One pack of bonito flakes a go!"

"What a bargain!"

It was such a cheap price to pay for Tsubasa Hanekawa's chastity! If that was really the offering price, I'd pay sixty years' worth up front for an exclusive contract!

"What's the myatter? Then one catnip…no, one cat food!"

"Change the unit all you want, it won't matter. You need to say a number bigger than one! Or can you only count that high?!"

Hmm.

What a strange feeling.

I was conversing normally with someone I'd put my life on the line fighting not too long ago, over Golden Week… Then again—aberrations were all about how you approached them. How you dealt with them…I guessed.

"You're kind of a nyasty person, treating me like an idiot… Fine then, human! It's time to decide who's the bigger idiot!"

"Why would I want to do something that pointless?!"

"The event will be a match of shogi!"

"If two idiots faced off in a serious shogi match, the result would be so lame it'd hurt to watch!"

Shogi chess.

As far as contests of skill that everyone knows how to play but few have mastered, shogi was right up there with baseball in Japan.

"Hmm. Then how about this? A game where whoever pawses a stopwatch at purrsisely one second wins!"

"How dull can you get?!"

And wait.

You couldn't measure intelligence that way.

I picked my bike up off the ground… Trusty old granny bike that it was, it was oddly sturdy, suffering only a bent basket. Nothing was broken.

"All right," I said, "I think we should walk around looking for her together after I park my bike somewhere around here… It'll be slower going, but we'd be more thorough that way. Okay?"

"Meow."

"Her blond hair won't make her any easier to find with human eyes now that it's this dark out…so I'm counting on you, okay?"

"Count on me!"

I began walking, pushing my bike along. Black Hanekawa followed behind me…no, she overtook me and walked in the front, as if to lead. She really was a stupid cat… Maybe some instinct made her want to run past anything that moved.

The cat and the aberration were inseparable—apparently.

In that sense, I could call the cat monster the easiest aberration of all to understand—it was definitely the best-known one I had encountered until that point, aside from vampires. Well, I got cat monsters in general, but I, with my limited information, hadn't heard of the identifier that was "Afflicting Cat" until Golden Week.

Hmm, but I wondered… What would it look like if an objective bystander saw me walking alongside Black Hanekawa? A high school boy walking alongside a young, cat-eared maiden…how would they see me? No one could ever think the cat ears were real, and walking around in her pajamas was way better than walking around in her underwear, but… Maybe it would've been a good idea to head back to the abandoned cram school for now to grab her hat and blouse.

Then again, putting clothes on any beast, not just a cat, was a Herculean undertaking... It was a miracle in itself that she hadn't taken off those pajamas...

Oh, whatever.

It wouldn't mean anything to worry about it now.

There were already rumors about me walking arm-in-arm with Suruga Kanbaru, our second-year star. Adding a rumor about me walking around with a cat-eared beauty to that didn't really change anything. I could deal with Kanbaru and Hachikuji, and though it'd be hard to come up with an excuse to tell Sengoku, you know, what happens happens. Our top priority now was to find Shinobu.

It was Hanekawa's honor I was concerned for if anything. Then again, the pajamas might just barely pass as street clothes, plus she had her glasses off, and she had a different hairstyle, and most importantly her hair had changed from black to white. No one would think I was with Hanekawa unless they knew what was going on. No amount of dye or bleach could do this good of a job on someone's hair color. Her facial expressions were totally different, too... Even I didn't know who Black Hanekawa was when I first saw her during Golden Week. If not for the shape of her hips—no, it was only because she'd saved my life that I was somehow able to pin down her identity.

Plus.

This was also—Tsubasa Hanekawa.

Another Hanekawa.

She had two sides, and this was the reverse side.

"Hey, human," Black Hanekawa said from the front. "Refresh my meowmory. What was it ya wanted me to do again?"

"..............."

The intelligence of a cat...

Should I be relying on her?

We reached a bookstore after walking for a bit—the bookstore that boasted the largest selection in town, the same one where Hanekawa and I had picked out study aids together the other day. The store was still open...so while it pained me to park my bike there when I wasn't going to be doing any shopping, I had no choice. I decided to put it there.

We departed once again.

Still no traces of Shinobu's scent.

Speaking of scents, I could imagine a cat's sense of smell being better than a human's, but how much better was it, if you were to quantify it? Not as good as a dog's, I assumed.

"Hey, human."

"What is it, cat monster."

"Seems a lot happened after ya battled it out with me—between you and *us*."

"What, did Oshino tell you?"

Did he talk to her while he kept watch?

It would be like him. He did like to talk.

"Yeah," I said. "A crab, a snail, a monkey, and a snake."

"That myakes a Nue!"

"Only the monkey and snake part… What about the crab and the snail, where did those go? And wait, stop saying whatever pops into your head."

My impression of Hanekawa was growing worse and worse.

I wished she'd show me at least a glimpse of her intelligence.

"And I'm—a demon."

"Hm. Meow," Black Hanekawa said. "Human—you call *us* aberrations, but…what do ya think about them?"

"What do I think about them?"

So her nocturnal nature did make her a little more coherent at night… It was the same way last time, too—but the changes weren't drastic.

What could the question mean?

It was a vaguely worded sentence.

"Well, human, if ya think you've gotten nyused to us—I need to drag ya by the scruff back to reality. Aberrations are aberrations, humans are humans—nyever together. They can't get along, nyo matter what."

"I…don't really understand. What is it you're trying to tell me?"

"Well, that's because you're stupid."

"No one could hurt me more with those words than you!"

"Hmph. You nyow what they say about hurt feelings... Meow? Err, what do they say."

"Don't run your mouth if you can't come up with anything! It's painful to watch someone incapable of a snappy line trying to say something smart!"

Our conversation was going nowhere.

What were we even talking about, anyway?

"So are you trying to say that it's impossible for me to get used to aberrations? I guess I do feel that way... I'm left speechless and looking like a loser every time I deal with one. It's as pathetic as it gets. Things never go for me like they do for Oshino."

Mèmè Oshino.

A professional—an authority on transformed creatures.

It was strange when I thought about it. How did he ever start down that path? I knew next to nothing about his background. Oh, maybe he said something about having gone to a Shinto university... But I didn't know how much of his resume I could believe. He was the sort who made things up to suit the occasion.

"Nyo, that's nyot what I want to say—for example, human. Can ya imagine why that vampire could've hightailed it?"

"...Not at all."

"Ah. So that's how little ya understyand about us... And that's purrobably why Hawaiian shirt tends to be right. He—nyows the difference."

"Knows the differ—"

"He nyows what he's nyot."

"..............."

Offer a hand without knowing what you're doing—and you'll get burned.

Was that what she meant?

I hadn't just offered a hand, I'd offered my neck. In that case, there really wasn't anything I could do. I was at the whim of the waves—I couldn't claim to have gotten used to anything.

Especially—when it came to Shinobu.

A legendary vampire—descended from a noble bloodline.

"Did you—hear about me and Shinobu from Oshino? You say all that, but do you really understand our relationship?"

"Nyot that well—I may have heard, but I already furgot. I don't understand, to say the least."

"Well, that's awfully casual of you."

"Maybe, but I get it in large part—but when I say 'large part,' I'm not meowing about my myaster's breasts, mrowkay?!"

"……"

I couldn't detect the slightest bit of intelligence from that joke…

She wasn't being dirty, she was just being vulgar.

"Aberrations understand aberrations best—*we're the same, after all.*"

"The same…" They seemed like very different types of aberrations. They were the same in that both were inhuman? No, that wasn't it. "The same, being aberrations, huh?"

"I'm nyot saying anything difficult—I can't say anything difficult, anyway. Listen, human—that word 'aberration' says it all," Black Hanekawa asserted. "Aberrations—creatures that are *aberrant*, meow. *Different from humans*—that's why ya can't get used to us. If ya did, there'd be nyothing aberrant about us anymore. People need to believe in us, fear us, dread us, loathe us, revere us, respect us, hate us, shun us, and pray to us—that's why we exist."

"……………"

"But get used to us? Nyot gonna happen."

If you want to treat us like friends? Nyo thanks—

Is how Black Hanekawa summarized it.

For some reason, it felt like I'd been warned. But when I thought about it, she was right… The boundaries between us might have become fuzzy for me because I'd once become more than half aberrant myself. Being overly conscious of it was an issue—but not being conscious of it at all was also an issue.

Shinobu.

Somewhere down the line—hadn't I started treating her as a simple kid?

I'd never refer to her as human.

But—hadn't I been thinking of her that way?

187

"Hey... Wait, hold on... Don't tell me, is that why?"

"Meow?"

"It's because I saw Shinobu *in that kind of way*—*that Shinobu, as an aberration, decided to disappear?*"

A vampire.

But—a mockery of a vampire.

It would have been a challenge to her identity.

And strangely enough, Oshino had said something similar. A journey of self-discovery.

Did Shinobu—no longer know who she was?

She—couldn't comprehend herself.

"Purrhaps, or purrhaps not. I wouldn't know those kinds of details—I might be the same, but I'm also different. But, human, there's one thing you should remeowmber... What was it again?"

"You forgot it yourself!"

"Right, that's it. *We* might be here as a myatter of course—but as soon as people think that's a myatter of course, we become mere reality."

Demons—would be mere blood disorders.

Cats—would be mere multiple personalities.

Crabs—would be mere illnesses.

Snails—would be mere lost children.

Monkeys—would be mere slashers.

Snakes—would be mere pain.

Aberrations—would be mere reality.

"And we'd end up saying something dull like 'There's no room in our scientific society for aberrations'?"

"Nyope. *We just wouldn't be able to maintain the same forms*—we'll be here, always and forever. So long as you humans are around."

"And that's how—you've come all this way alongside humans."

"Purrcisely."

Precisely, she said—the Afflicting Cat.

"Still—I haven't gotten a sniff of her."

"Hm? Oh, you're talking about Shinobu's scent... No tracks, either?"

"I should pick up on it in nyo time at all, she's got a unique scent...

Hey, human. Are you sure that vampire really left?"

"Yeah... I'm sure of that much. She's been spotted at least once."

"Oh. So nyo chance she just purrtended to leave and hid inside those ruins..."

"That's pretty smart, coming from you... I never considered that one."

"What if she left once, then came back? That place is so full of her scent she could cameowflage herself there."

"I'm pretty sure Oshino would notice if that was the case..."

Camouflage—huh.

Hm? Hold on, I thought, I'm about to come upon something... What was it? I lost the thread... How could I complain about the cat monster at this rate? It really was going to become a contest to see who was the bigger idiot.

Did I have the intelligence of a cat?

Umm.

"Oh, right—why don't we try going to where Shinobu was spotted? It'll take us off this path, but we can head to the Mister Donut...and then we just have to follow Shinobu's scent from there."

"Hrmm. I'm nyot exactly following her scent, though—strictly speaking, I don't rely on the intensity of a scent."

"You don't?"

"To be honyest, I went to look for the vampire alone after sneaking out of the building—so I probably went by that Mister Donut, too."

"Seriously? You need to tell me that kind of thing sooner."

So we needed to change course. If we were searching for her scent, there was no point in searching a place that had already been searched.

"Sorry, I furgot."

".........."

Now I felt an urgent need to obstinately go back and forth along our path, checking it again and again.

"The scent...vanished along the way," Black Hanekawa said.

"Vanished?"

"It wasn't possible to follow her any further... So, human. A question. How much of her vampire powers can that vampire use right nyow? If she can disappear, reappear, and turn into shadows and darkness—then I'll be honest. I won't be able to find her."

"It's safe to assume that she can barely use any of her powers as a vampire right now. They're close to entirely limited—and even if she somehow manages to use them, she only can when I'm around. She'd be able to do a little bit, since I fed her my blood at the beginning of this week, but if I'm not around, she's just—"

Just a kid.

Not an aberration.

Reality.

But that understanding—was wrong?

"Hmm. In that case…" Black Hanekawa muttered to herself. She seemed to be thinking, not that it would do her any good. "But if we look at it that way, it's nyot very…"

"What is it? Stop leaving me out of this. We have a saying in our world, you know. 'Gather three men and you shall have the wisdom of prajñā—"

"I see. What's prajñyā?"

"………"

What could it be?

I'd been using the word without ever knowing.

"There aren't three of us, anyway," she said.

"Yeah, you're right."

"*One man and one cat*—meow."

Not two men—one man and one cat.

She wasn't saying that because she could only count to one—right?

"Anyway—human. Nyow I don't think that vampire can be found with just ordinary meowthods."

"So she might have left town? I know this is just the flip side of what I just said, but well, if she's that far away from me, I don't think she—"

I'd be going too far if I said she couldn't do anything.

But if she tried, there was a possibility she'd no longer be able to maintain her existence.

"The reason vampires suck blood—meow."

"What?"

"Vampires suck human blood—but it means different things when they suck it for food and when they suck it to make companyans."

"......"

I knew that.

I heard that during spring break—but why did this cat know? She only had the intellect of a cat... Oh, of course. Intelligence was different from knowledge. Despite the difference between Hanekawa and Black Hanekawa's intellects, they probably shared some knowledge.

"Myaybe that's why she ran off..."

"Huh? How so?"

"...Mrow, you're so dense," Black Hanekawa said, sounding flabbergasted.

"Dense? What do you mean?"

"I'm saying you're obtuse."

"Well, I'll agree I'm not the best at reading people's minds..."

"I'm saying you're obtusely angled."

"Don't tell me you're going to need a protractor."

"I'm saying that ever since she met ya during spring break or whenever, that vampire has seen ya getting mixed up with one aberration after anyother. Myaybe that didn't feel so great."

"You mean, seeing all of those different aberrations, yourself included, made her feel less special? That's why she couldn't stand being around any longer—"

"So dense," Black Hanekawa repeated.

Dense... I didn't like the word, for some reason.

She added, "They say beasts separate themselves from humans when they realize the time has come for them to die—myaybe vampires are the same way?"

"Don't say ominous things like that."

"Are ya really mewing about omens to an aberration? But what are ya going to do if ya never find that vampire?"

"What am I going to do? Well, I'd be in trouble. Hanekawa wouldn't be able to turn back to normal, plus—"

"But that's the only problem? If you ignyore my myaster—wouldn't ya be better off if that vampire wasn't around?"

"……" What was she trying to say? It didn't make any sense to me.

"You still have the vague scent of a vampire because she exists. Ya let her drink your blood or something—that's what ya said, murright? So you can go back to being a simple human if the vampire disappears."

The demon—would be a mere human.

I could go back.

All I had to do was abandon Shinobu.

"You can't—expect me to do that. I could never abandon her. I—"

If Hanekawa was my savior.

Then Shinobu was my victim.

"She could kill me," I continued, "and I still wouldn't have any right to complain. What I did to her was that bad."

"You say that, but are ya sure ya just don't want to give up your immortal body?"

"That's not it. If she dies tomorrow, I'm ready for my life to last just as long."

"…Hm. I see."

You're seeing yourself in her, Black Hanekawa said.

If you're going to put it like that, then sure—it was just unilateral sentiment. I couldn't complain if Shinobu saw that as annoying or irritating.

Or maybe that was why—

It could have been why Shinobu left.

"Also, cat. The premise of your hypothesis is flawed to begin with. How could I 'ignore' your master? It's impossible. Sorry, but we need to get you back into her deepest reaches—I'm not going to have another Golden Week."

"Oh. But, human—I wouldn't say it's impossible at all. There's a way to get me back deep inside of her without relying on that vampire at all."

"…There is?"

There was a way?

If it was quick—that's exactly what I wanted.

Ten days was our limit—in other words, it'd be fine so long as we could bring everything to a resolution within nine days in the worst case, just like last time.

"If ya want to talk about Golden Week, it was the same then, too. I'm a nyavatar of my myaster's stress—get rid of the root of the stress, and I'll disappear once again."

"Hmm..."

When this Afflicting Cat sent Hanekawa's parents to the hospital using her energy drain, Hanekawa became aware of what was going on as herself for a brief moment—probably because what she'd done considerably relieved the stress she felt. It wasn't enough in the end, given all the stress that had piled up and up inside of her, so Black Hanekawa reappeared right afterwards—

So. The root of her stress.

"Oshino brought that up too, but we don't have the time to pin down the root," I said. "It doesn't seem to be her family drama this time, plus—"

"Why would ya need to pin anything down? I nyow what it is."

"...Oh, right."

I'd carelessly overlooked that fact.

If she was the avatar of Hanekawa's stress, then she'd know the nature of that stress and what the stressor was better than anyone, even Hanekawa herself. That was exactly why she'd attacked Hanekawa's parents first—

"Wait, but that still leaves us with an issue, cat. Even if we do learn what the stressor is, we don't have any way to get rid of it. It'd become Hanekawa's issue at that point, so—"

You can't solve another person's worries.

Just like with Hanekawa's parents—there was nothing I could do.

It was the same for other worries.

"So it doesn't matter what the stressor is...though I admit I'm curious to know. Is it about what she's doing after graduation, given the timing? Come to think of it, it seems like she had a headache when we were talking about post-graduation plans at the bookstore, too—it sounded like she knew what she wanted to do, but maybe in her heart she actually—"

"It's nyot about graduation."

"It isn't?"

"Anyway—I think you in purrticular could easily resolve her distress, and all this stress."

"Easily?"

"Mice and easy."

"Would Hanekawa get distressed over something that's so easy to resolve? Or I guess its simplicity could be what's giving her such a hard time... Hm? Hold on, cat. What do you mean, me in particular?"

If I could do it—couldn't anyone?

But in that case, once again, would she really get distressed over—something that anyone could fix? If there was something I could do, Hanekawa herself would be able to as well—

I suddenly glanced at the watch on my right wrist.

More time had passed.

Senjogahara would have to be back home by now—but she did say she planned to bring work home with her, so the real struggle was only getting started. Now that I thought about it, Senjogahara was probably the only one in our class who could handle what Hanekawa had been dealing with... It seemed like Hanekawa's eye for people was spot-on even when she had cat ears growing out of her head.

An eye for people, eh.

But if that was true, her eyes must have been shut when she installed me as class vice president... Doing that had essentially doubled her workload. Then again, you could increase her workload tenfold, and she'd probably handle it with ease—

"Well, ya see, human. My myaster," Black Hanekawa said, sounding a bit cagey, "she's in love with ya."

"...Huh?"

"So if ya love my myaster back, I should be able to get out of the way, but—meow? What's the myatter?"

"......Um."

My feet halted.

Actually—my brain did, too.

What was that supposed to mean?

"Are you trying to be funny or something? I can't come up with a

194

quip for every stupid setup, you know… And if that's a joke, it's really too nasty. You need to know there are some things you can lie about and some things that you shouldn't—"

"You're such a fool, human. Is this the face of someone who can tell a lie?"

"………"

It wasn't.

To be honest, I hated the old line, "If I was going to lie to you, I'd tell a more believable lie" (some lies anticipated you'd assume so), but in this case, the Afflicting Cat didn't have the ability to lie to begin with. I've never lied before in my life—Hanekawa told me once, but this was the diametric opposite.

The Afflicting Cat couldn't lie.

Which meant.

"B-But…" I stammered. "If you're not lying, cat, then you must be mistaken. There's no way that could be true."

"What makes ya think that? How could I ever misunderstand my myaster. She's my one and only myaster."

"But Hanekawa…"

She was kind to everyone.

The worse someone was as a person, the more sympathy she showed.

That's why—she picked me, of all people.

And that's why—during spring break, too.

"You only understand things that have to do with her stress," I argued. "I know you might share her knowledge, but there must be some things you can't access. It's impossible. Why would Hanekawa—"

No.

Then again, Senjogahara had once tried to trick me into telling her how I felt about Hanekawa—back when Senjogahara was like a mass of self-defensiveness and caution. If that Senjogahara tested a hunch, wasn't there some basis to it?

"Yesss, and that's what I'm saying," Black Hanekawa stated as though she were teaching a slow student how to use a calculator. "*That's what the stress was*—my myaster is in love with ya, but you're dating someone else. And ya've been—flaunting it."

"………"

Headaches—starting about a month ago.

So she said.

A month ago from now would be—right, Mother's Day. The day Senjogahara and I started going out—and *Hanekawa knew about us from that very day—*

The class president—there was nothing she didn't know.

She knew everything.

"But Hanekawa never acted that way—if anything, it was like she was cheering us on, giving me advice and stuff—"

"*That's exactly why* the stress kept building up. Do ya really think my myaster would ever be able to snyatch away a taken man? She's fair and just, clean and pure, she values harmony over everything—she thinks it's nyatural to sacrifice herself for the sake of others. She wouldn't ever breathe a word."

Love means never having to say sorry—

But.

Not everyone could do that.

So I was asking someone like that for advice and having her cheer me on? It was the same when I had to deal with Kanbaru, too, and even when we were at the bookstore, it wasn't just graduation we were talking about, but Senjogahara—I was choosing what to do next with her in mind—

Hanekawa's headaches didn't abate—

They only got worse and worse.

"………"

I felt—sick.

What had I done?

But how could I have noticed… I mean, Hanekawa? If that woman made a serious attempt to hide her own feelings, even Senjogahara wouldn't be able to suss them out.

But.

Dense—huh.

So her plans after graduation, too… Oshino must have had some influence on her, but you could also look at it as Tsubasa Hanekawa's

196

grand heartbreak journey—and she started showing signs of a headache right after we talked about post-graduation plans.

Plus.

There was the time she closed her eyes, her lips turned up to me—

"When—did it start?"

"Around spring break. I dunno exactly what her heart was going through then, since it was before I ever appeared, but my myaster was living in an environment that put her under constant stress. Your story of humans and vampires was so purrposterous that ya must have seemed to have the power to break her out of her predicament."

"Break her out?"

How could I?

My hands were so full then that—

"Though I don't think you could say there were nyo signs at all. My myaster was close to perfect when it came to that—but she must have let her guard down here and there since it was a myatter of love. Ya never found it odd that a dead-serious class president would choose a vice president like you? Any nyormal person would realize that was a wrong pick."

"Oh… Well."

Yes, she had picked the wrong person for the job.

There'd been a reason.

"Assuming you were a delinquent and trying to rehabilitate ya sounds like a reason that's not much of a reason at all."

"That's—"

Back then—in early April, when Hanekawa appointed me as her vice president after half-pushing her recommendation through a decent amount of opposition—her pick generated a fair amount of backlash. I was so intimately involved in the affair that I didn't see it that way then, and I'd unreservedly bought Hanekawa's line that people mature when they're put in positions of responsibility. But actually, didn't she hate that kind of push by way of authority more than anything?

"Then why?"

"Why else? Because she wanted to be with ya as much as possible. Third-year class presidents and vice presidents get to work together to prepare for the last culture festival of their high school lives, meowfter all... But she stopped trying that on ya a month ago. The romyance my myaster slowly built up and up, one piece at a time—ended there. Myaa-haha, no, should I say that's when it really got started?"

"........"

When it happened, Hanekawa—was happy for me.

Or so I thought.

But—that was another lie?

She'd never lied before in her life? Uh-uh.

If this was true, Tsubasa Hanekawa, you've been lying through your teeth!

"To be honyest, I think my myaster was careless. She all but nyever thought a rival would ever appear. If only my myaster had known that *you're kind to everyone* the same way ya were to her during Golden Week—if only she'd considered that someone else might get saved by you just like she was, I know my myaster is smart enough to have acted sooner. The woman you're dating didn't waste a meowment in comparison, right?"

"Yeah, that's true..."

Senjogahara—didn't hesitate.

She went in for the kill as soon as she made up her mind.

To the point that the normal reaction was to feel creeped out.

"A girl raised in a cold and loveless home," narrated Black Hanekawa. "During spring break, she encountered something shocking and unusual, and that something also happened to be her classmate. It felt almost like fate. Feelings of love started to bud. And then her own life was saved by that classmate—turning that love into something certain. Or something. Nyaa-hahahaha, ya know, my myaster would obviously be the purrtagonist if it were a girls' myanga—but the way it all got snyatched away from her, I don't know if I should call it purrfect or pathetic."

"No one strikes faster than Senjogahara—she could start later than everyone else and not even think of it as a handicap."

Or—

She moved with almost hasty speed on Mother's Day because she was sensitive enough to Hanekawa's intentions even to be testing a hunch. That might also explain the strange distance she maintained vis-à-vis Hanekawa—but.

That wasn't Senjogahara's fault.

That kind of thing isn't a competition to begin with.

"Whatever the case, it's all too late nyow. My myaster isn't the kind of person who could ever steal from anyother, but how pure. It was supposed to be the kind of love you read about in girls' myanga, but it turned into longing for a taken man in nyo time flat, ending up as an illicit, and unrequited, love…and she felt guilty about it, meow."

"Well, she's—a serious person."

She couldn't be open about how head over heels she was about someone, unlike Sengoku's tormentor. But that didn't mean coming to a neat compromise with her feelings, either. She wasn't the kind of person who could bargain and settle with herself.

"She must have had her regrets, too—if only she'd confessed her feelings sooner…" observed Black Hanekawa. "But it's nyot an early cat gets the bird kind of thing, and humans who think that way are petty, ridiculous, and boring—"

But.

She never breathed a word about it.

She cheered me on—and lent me an ear when I needed advice.

Is that what had been going on?

All the time she was cheering me on and giving me advice, she was talking about her own feelings—

Of course she would have opinions regarding the subtleties of romance and relations between the sexes.

A girl in love would—she'd have understood how Senjogahara felt better than anyone else.

"That's also why you triggered my myaster's stress during Golden Week. You might have been the one person she didn't want knowing—meow."

"Then—"

Be there when she needed me? Far from it.

At that moment, I was the last person she needed, the greatest hindrance.

"You're so dense that you didn't show any signs of nyoticing my myaster's affection or her turmoil, and her stress just continued to build—if you ask me, I'm impressed she lasted a month."

"Wait, cat. Hold on. Are you sure—that's right? Even if you're right and I was the cause of her stress—"

If I wasn't merely the trigger during Golden Week, but also the very bullet that tore through her guts—

"That wouldn't be enough to make you appear, would it? I was only part of it at most, and there must have been some other powerful stressor that—"

"Nyope. It was all you," Black Hanekawa declared. "As far as her parents go—my myaster considers that somewhat settled after Golden Week. Ya might not understand, though."

"But that doesn't make sense. You're the incarnation of the stress that kept building up inside of her because of her family. If it was only over a couple of months of romance, why would you—"

"Only?" The cat's eyes—shone forebodingly. She made no effort to hide her irritation. "Is there some reason a few months of exacerbated heartbreak shouldn't be allowed to surpass ten-odd years of family strife?"

I haven't led the happiest life up until now... But I think I could call it all even if I see it as what let me meet you.

If it was my unhappiness that caught your attention—then I'm glad it happened that way.

Those were Senjogahara's words.

But—then again.

Did such things really happen?

"You look like ya don't get it, human... Could it actually be that you've never really fallen in love with anybody?"

"Wha..."

"Are ya sure you're not just going out with that girl because that's what she insisted on? If so, you oughta break up right away and go out with my myaster instead. That would make me disappear, too. You'd be just as happy dating anyone, wouldn't ya?"

"......"

Maybe I should have gotten angry here—maybe I shouldn't have stayed silent after being so blatantly provoked. And really, if I hadn't been talking to someone who looked like Tsubasa Hanekawa—I think I would have.

But—it was Hanekawa saying this.

I felt like I had no right to get angry.

"...I can't do that, cat."

"Hrrm? Why nyot? You think of my myaster as your savior—so shouldn't you be repaying the favor? At the end of the day, are your feelings of love more important than your feelings of gratitude?"

"If I let that happen—Hanekawa would be taking advantage of my gratitude. I'm not going to put her in that position... No, that's not it. That's just a convenient excuse. It's simpler than that, I can't lie about my feelings for Senjogahara. And even if I did, wouldn't Hanekawa see right through it?"

I'm bad at telling lies, and I'm bad at hiding things.

I'm flimsy and weak.

I couldn't deceive Hanekawa even if I wanted—I didn't want to, of course, and while a part of me might have wanted to if I could, just to do it, I couldn't.

"It's not an issue of me accepting it and sticking it out," I said. "There really isn't a thing I can do about it—right? It's not like Hanekawa would want to go out with me if I was doing that, either..."

"Is that so? Actually, I felt myself fading a teeny bit just now when I told ya how my myaster feels—it's clearly relieving her of her stress. No one's beautiful through and through, nyot even my myaster. *See how I lurk beneath her.* You myight be surprised, maybe she'd love it and wouldn't mind at all. It could be painful at first, but completely fine once she's used to it."

"Once she's used to it—are you really saying that? If it were that simple, Hanekawa wouldn't have worried you all the way into existence. She's not the kind of person who could push someone aside for her own sake. She couldn't put herself ahead of another person. It's that fact about her—that makes me feel so indebted. I probably would have said yes before Mother's Day. Yes, I cared for her then, as a friend. But I can't do it now. My feelings are frozen in place for just one person now, and it's Senjogahara. You asked me if love is more important to me than gratitude, but—I can't put either one ahead of the other. It's a double bind. That's why I can't choose Hanekawa."

Wouldn't the normal choice between the two be Miss Hanekawa— that's what Hachikuji said. She wondered why I chose Miss Senjogahara—it struck her as odd.

Why.

How was I supposed to answer that one?

"It's everything about Senjogahara, including her personality, that I love."

I spoke the sentence in full.

Yes.

I love everything about her.

There's not a part of her that I don't love.

"It's the first time in my life I've really fallen in love with someone."

"Hmm. Really nyow."

Black Hanekawa backed down—casually.

Like she knew from the start what I was going to say.

Maybe she did—she was Hanekawa.

Maybe she saw it all coming.

She knows everything.

No—not everything.

Only what she knows.

"And also, cat—even if a few months of exacerbated heartbreak surpassed ten-odd years of family strife…that still isn't a reason for her to bring you out. She should have endured those headaches, like it or not. And not just this time, but during Golden Week, too—she relied on you out of weakness."

She may not have been flimsy—but weakness was weakness.

Even if it wasn't the result she wanted.

The weakness she ran to was the aggressor's.

"It's not you who should be saying those words to me, it's Hanekawa—all she did was force the hard work on you."

Like the time with Sengoku's snake.

That's what I did to Kanbaru.

Putting off a painful decision—and entrusting it to someone else.

That was just—having your cake and eating it too.

"You're an Afflicting Cat—an aberration. But an aberration that appeared out of Hanekawa's weakness. She may not have wished for what you gave her—but what you gave her was what she wanted. Everything you did, Hanekawa did. I know, of course...Hanekawa has her reasons. And I know this isn't something I should be saying, given that I share some responsibility for both times—but I'm pretty sure there are people in similar environments who manage to get out of them on their own, without relying on any aberration. The fact that Hanekawa relied on *something like you* is an insult to all of them."

"Well, well. Listen to you," Black Hanekawa sneered at me. "I guess ya have a right to say that—it's okay for you. You're a kind soul who'd even *sacrifice himself to save a vampire on the brink of death*."

"......"

"Being kind to everyone means ya don't have anyone special—I know, because my myaster is kind to everyone, too. Hmph. Well, okay, nyothing I can do. Ya can't change someone's feelings—I found that out last time. I found out, and learned."

"I'm glad to hear that." So we were just going to have to find Shinobu, after all. No surprise that there was no convenient solution. "But...I wonder if it's also the case for Hanekawa. If it is, then attacking her like I just did might be a little harsh..."

"Hrm? Whatcha talking about?"

"Oh, you know—I might be a mockery of one, but I'm still kind of like a vampire. And vampires have this ability, the power of fascination...which is why I've been so popular with girls ever since spring break. You must know about this, Hanekawa was the one who told me."

"We might share knowledge, but we don't share meowmories. Like ya said, I only know about things related to her stress."

"Oh, right."

Still, I was already a vampire when I met Hanekawa. And not any mockery, either—it was before I became human again, during my genuine, full-fledged vampire days—you couldn't begin to compare my powers of fascination and whatever else now to the ones I had then. Hanekawa fell face-first into the middle of that.

"She's a serious girl," I said. "If that's why she started brooding over me, I think it'd make her a complete victim—"

"………"

"What's wrong? Why'd you go quiet?"

"Nyo—that's nyot true," replied Black Hanekawa. "Yes, it's true that vampires can charm people—but even among true vampires, only certain types have that ability. So there's nyo way a knockoff vampire like you, who went from human to vampire, could ever use it."

"What? But—"

"And fascination isn't like some handy love potion ya might see in a myanga, anyway. The targets lose control of their will. It's the power to make puppets out of people."

"Make—puppets out of them? Not fascinate them?"

"Tell me, human. Is there a girl around you who's purrfectly obedient to your orders? Someone that does exactly what ya tell them, never once defying you?"

"………"

There wasn't a single person like that.

There absolutely wasn't.

Even Sengoku, the most docile of the bunch, inflicted unthinkable acts on me like handing me volleyball shorts and a school swimsuit in front of my own high school's gates.

But was the aberration saying that based on Hanekawa's knowledge? After all, it was Hanekawa herself who'd told me—

That was mean of me, wasn't it.

Oh…that's what she meant.

It was a lie.

A lie—something she claimed never to tell.

In that case, I knew what that meant about me and Senjogahara—but Hanekawa, too.

But given what I now knew, it seemed less like a case of being mean than a sort of lament—Tsubasa Hanekawa's doleful wish for that to have been our reality. She'd have been able to relieve some of her stress had it been the case—because she could blame it on an outside force.

But there was no one else for her to blame.

"Ya can't change someone's feelings—meow. I see, though. That wasn't like my myaster to do. Hmph, looks like not being able to lie caused me to let the cat out of the bag."

"I guess it's another instance of forcing the hard work on you."

It wasn't a good thing. The relief I felt, though, overshadowed that. It wasn't thanks to any vampire's, any aberration's power, it was me, as myself—

It was because I'm Koyomi Araragi.

"So—I can feel proud."

"Hrm?"

"That Hanekawa fell in love with me—"

What was that if not an honor?

I felt like that fact alone was enough to keep me going.

But to think that things would turn out like this… What would I have to do, at this point, to repay Hanekawa?

"Well, for now, we need to focus on tucking you away—damn it, where *did* Shinobu run off to? I haven't heard a word from anyone helping, either… Oh, and I need to order Sengoku to pull back soon…"

Wait, how would I do that?

She didn't have a cell phone.

Oh no. She could use a pay phone to contact me, but I had no way to contact her… What was I going to do? She could be stubborn in her own weird way, so she wasn't going to head home of her own accord without finding Shinobu, no matter how late it got…

Maybe…Kanbaru?

I could get her to temporarily stop looking for Shinobu and try to find Sengoku instead. Was that going to be it? Agh, why was I always having to rely on her when it mattered the most… I wouldn't ever be able to pay Kanbaru back at this rate. I was feeling ready to do anything she told me.

"Hey, human." I had my cell phone in hand as Black Hanekawa spoke to me. Her tone seemed somehow different from every utterance she'd made so far. "There's—one more way."

"One more?"

"A quick and effective way to get me back in there without relying on any vampire—the easiest way is for ya to date my myaster, but this might be the second easiest."

"I have my doubts about any plans you and your brain would come up with…but I'll listen. What is it?"

"Walk for me a bit. Over there, to below that street lamp."

"Like this?"

I did as she said.

I wasn't getting my hopes up, but I needed to try any plan I could get my hands on. Still, I didn't see what moving a dozen feet would do.

"Ah, a little to the front. You'd be right below it otherwise."

"Right below?"

I tilted my head as she continued to talk nonsensically, but still took a step forward—and then.

She embraced me from behind.

There was no sound of her footsteps—there was no sound at all.

She had moved like a cat on the hunt.

She passed both of her arms under my armpits and wrapped them around my torso—and held me. A sabaori, no, a sabaori is done from the front, and it's used to bring an opponent to his knees, not to crush his internal organs—and.

It's not used to drain an opponent's energy.

And instantaneously—it was being absorbed.

Whatever clothes we may have been wearing didn't matter.

Those two large cushions didn't matter.

I could rapidly feel my entire body weakening.

"C-Cat—you—"

I didn't have the energy to turn my head toward her. I didn't even feel like I could scream the way Hachikuji had when I'd done the same to her that morning.

I couldn't lift a pinkie.

But I didn't need to look behind me to know—it was Black Haneka-wa holding me. My moving away from her had been a ruse—all she wanted was for me to turn my back to her—

To let my guard down.

So she could suck me dry.

"Remember what I said? Don't ever think ya've gotten nyused to us. Humans can't ever get along with *us*, nyo matter what."

"Guh… Urgh, urrg—"

"The more we play nyice with you humans, the worse off we are— looks like we know who the bigger idiot is nyow."

It was true—I hated to admit it, but the Afflicting Cat was right.

The situation was already hopeless. I could never put up a fight against the Afflicting Cat even if I faced her head-on. All I had were some lingering aftereffects of being an aberration, I had no means to oppose an actual one. But to make it worse, she had come from behind—

It seemed ridiculous.

It seemed past ridiculous.

"B-But—what are you trying to do? Why do this to me here and now? It's not as if absorbing just me would get rid of Hanekawa's stress—"

"Like I said, it's one more plan—about the second easiest. Of course, it's the sharpest one from my purrspective," Black Hanekawa said—before *slurp*, licking my nape. I say lick, but the feeling wasn't what I'd call sensual—cat tongues are barbed in order to scrape meat from bones. The skin on my neck was torn from my flesh, and I could feel my blood gushing.

The cat monster drank that blood—and laughed.

"*You're the cause of the stress—it's you who's the stressor. Get rid of you,* and I don't nyeed to be here anymore. It's not 'just you' I'm absorbing— you're the only one I nyeed. Ya myight nyot be able to change someone's feelings—but you can erase someone's existence."

"Th-That's—"

Her ability to drain energy.

There'd been no case of it being bad enough to kill someone—but that by no means meant that it couldn't. No human could have their energy and their core exhausted—and continue living.

But…would this make your master happy, Black Hanekawa?

"My myaster doesn't remember anything I do—okay? She won't think of it as something she did herself. She'll be sad if you're gone, of course, but even then—it'd be better than now. I can feel it—sucking ya dry like this is making me fade away—"

"I-I thought you said you'd learned—after you attacked Hanekawa's parents over Golden Week… It still wasn't enough? A person's stress isn't that simple of a—"

"Nyo, that's nyot it—my mistake then was nyot killing my myaster's parents. I went wrong when I tried to be considerate in some weird way to my myaster—not killing anybody was what I did wrong. That's what I learned. And I'm nyot going to make the same mistake again—I'm killing you nyo matter what."

"Kill me…"

I couldn't believe the words.

I couldn't believe the words were coming out of Hanekawa's mouth—but perhaps even these were her own, coming from somewhere inside of her.

Flip it around, and the reverse was the obverse.

In that case.

Hanekawa, in fact—might feel happy about this. *She'd never wish for this to happen*—that thought might have been nothing more than an illusion I projected on her. It could have been—the result she wanted. She might be getting this—because it's what she wished for. The Afflicting Cat's earlier proposal of going out with Hanekawa, even if it meant lying, had to have come from somewhere inside of her.

In that case.

"…Hanekawa."

In that case—this would be a good way.

She'd saved my life.

I'd do anything for her sake.

I may not be able to change how I feel—

But I could think that I wouldn't mind dying.

"Ya oughta be happy—ya get to die in the embrace of my myaster's naughty body. Nyow shrivel in bliss."

"……"

It was going to be hard for me to feel that way while all of the feeling was leaving my body—and anyway, my most immediate sensation was the pain in my torso—from the sharp claws at the end of those arms around me stabbing into my abs—but even then.

If I could die for Hanekawa's sake.

"........."

No—I couldn't.

I couldn't do it.

There was what Senjogahara had said—so I couldn't let myself be killed. If Hanekawa killed me—or even if Hanekawa's body killed me, Senjogahara would kill her in turn. This was no projected illusion, this was certainty. Senjogahara wouldn't hesitate, I knew that. And there'd be no way to prevent it when it came to that. Senjogahara wouldn't even give Hanekawa the time to feel stressed.

So—I couldn't do it.

This was the absolute worst way possible.

"L-Let me go."

"Hrrm?"

"Just—let me go."

I didn't have room to explain. The Afflicting Cat didn't know Senjogahara—no, she'd have had some knowledge of her, but Hanekawa's knowledge of Senjogahara was limited. Unless you knew her as well as I did, or at least as well as Kanbaru did, you wouldn't recognize the danger Hitagi Senjogahara posed...but I'd be like a sheet of paper floating in the wind by the time I spelled it all out.

"Begging for your life? That's good—I wouldn't mind letting ya free if ya say you'll go out with my myaster."

"Gah... Like I said, that's impossible—"

"I thought as myuch," Black Hanekawa said—casually, once again. "Fine, then. Just die."

"........."

"Or do ya want to try asking someone for help? You've saved so many people up until now—maybe someone myight come save you."

"Someone?"

Like who?

Hachikuji? Sengoku? Kanbaru? Senjogahara?

"There's no way—anyone could save me."

"No? Why nyot?"

"Because people just go and get saved on their own—"

"That's nyot your own opinyan, is it?" she retorted, gently. "Those are just words—nyot how you feel. If you're just parroting the words of others, it barely means a thing—the question is how *you* feel, meow."

"…Guh, gurrh—"

"Yes, people do go and get saved on their own—but why should people who help others care? They can go and save as many people as they please." The cat's voice was throaty. "Tell me, how many people do ya think are out there—who want to help you? And are ya gonna reject every single one of 'em—?"

The strength—left my body.

I couldn't stay standing anymore.

It was like Black Hanekawa's arms, wrapped around my body, were the only thing supporting me—like I'd entrusted my body to her completely.

My mind grew hazy, too.

I could do nothing.

I could do nothing—on my own.

It made me want to laugh, but I didn't have the strength for that, either. I didn't have the strength—but still, I wanted to laugh.

Yeah.

I guess…she would be sad.

Hanekawa…and Senjogahara, too.

And Kanbaru, and Sengoku.

Maybe even Hachikuji.

If I died.

"Help…"

I mustered the words.

I mustered the words together—and spoke them.

"Help me…Shinobu."

At that moment.

A girl leapt out—from my own shadow.

A blonde.

A helmet with goggles on top.

She had a small build—but she tore Black Hanekawa's hug from my body in the blink of an eye. A breath later and she'd sent Black Hanekawa's body flying. The cat couldn't even turn its body in the air and slammed into the lamp on the opposite side of the street. The street-light bent—no, it wasn't that hard, but the impact was enough to make it sway.

Then she landed.

Shinobu Oshino leapt out from the shadows—

And landed as she shook her blond hair everywhere she pleased.

Shinobu.

She was hiding…there?

But when I thought about it—that was about the only possible place left. It was unthinkable not to have received so much as a report of a sighting after searching this town for so long—and the Afflicting Cat's sense of smell shouldn't have failed so utterly.

So.

I should have assumed what followed, that she was using *some kind* of vampire ability—but I'd convinced myself that she couldn't because her abilities were limited.

No.

There was a hole in my logic.

I'd known, hadn't I? *She could use a little bit of her powers if she was near me*—which meant *she had to be hiding near me*. That was all there was to it.

A psychological blind spot—one of the fundamentals of the mystery novel.

If you want to hide something, hide it in plain view.

Not only that, the hiding spot was extremely effective against a cat's sense of smell, too—*because the scent would be masked by mine*.

My thin shadow—

Shinobu took advantage of that.

It was probably in the afternoon—or maybe the morning. As I was looking for Shinobu—she found me first. To make a random guess, I'd say it was around the Mister Donut. And that's where Shinobu—hid in my shadow. She belonged to the world of darkness, and hiding in someone's shadow was a vampire specialty—but that was the old her. Now mine might have been the only shadow she could hide in—

Oh.

Right below it—that's what she meant.

Because that would cause my shadow to be directly below me—so telling me to go under the streetlight… It was obvious who would win in a fight between an Afflicting Cat and a mockery of a human like me, and there was no need for her to go to the trouble of attacking me from behind. She didn't have to toy around with any complicated plans, she needed only to attack me fair and square.

Which meant—

I looked over to Black Hanekawa as she lay crumpled under the streetlight.

Black Hanekawa—grinned.

But that too was only for a moment.

Shinobu had no mercy—the moment after the Afflicting Cat landed, Shinobu sprung toward her and attacked. Extending her short limbs as far as they could go, she entwined them around Black Hanekawa's body—and *sunk her teeth* into her neck.

Black Hanekawa never stood a chance.

From there—Shinobu sucked.

If an Afflicting Cat had the ability to drain energy—so did a vampire. An eye for an eye, a tooth for a tooth, an aberration for an aberration, an energy drain for an energy drain. Even then, Shinobu's vitality was being sucked away by the Afflicting Cat simply because the two were touching—but Shinobu was sucking away even more vitality from the Afflicting Cat.

As utter food.

As aberrations, a vampire outclasses an Afflicting Cat, like night and day.

As aberrations, a vampire outclasses an Afflicting Cat night and day.

The scene was a rehash of what I witnessed during Golden Week—a perfect recreation. Though it took quite a suitable amount of effort that

212

time to force her into this position…Black Hanekawa wasn't fighting back this time.

Because she had neither the chance nor the will now.

While there was no way to prevent her always-on energy drain—the Afflicting Cat was surrendering to Shinobu. If the cat felt like it, she had the strength, endurance, and mobility to take on Shinobu as she was now (and only as she was now), and yet—

For Hanekawa.

It was for—her master.

Of course, I shouldn't pretend that I understood. Just as Black Hanekawa said, I couldn't act like I was used to them, too familiar or over-familiar—and I find it hard to believe that it was what Black Hanekawa wanted from the beginning.

While her intelligence might have been that of a cat, she must have realized that Shinobu could be hiding in my shadow—and also that there was no easy way to lure her out. To that end, she'd used me as bait, as a hostage, moving me under a street lamp where my shadow would be isolated even at night, before using her energy drain on me. That much was clear—but.

Black Hanekawa probably wouldn't have minded killing me. If Shinobu wasn't hiding in my shadow and truly had left town, Black Hanekawa probably would've been fine sucking up my entire existence.

It only happened to end up this way.

She didn't have the brain to tell a lie.

Everything the Afflicting Cat said—she meant.

It was how she really felt.

And—it was also how Hanekawa felt inside.

The hard work—that she was forcing on the Afflicting Cat.

She was right.

Looks like we knew—who the bigger idiot was now.

"…Ah."

Black Hanekawa's hair—gradually regained its color.

It turned gray, then brown—then black.

Her cat ears, too, slowly dwindled.

That existence, the aberration—was being sucked away by Shinobu.

Aberration slayer.

That was the curse spat at Shinobu until spring break.

Whether it was an Afflicting Cat or anything else, she sunk her fangs in and sucked—ripping its very existence out from the world. A genuine, full-fledged aberrant creature—

A vampire, the king of aberrations, the ruler of unlife.

"Time to stop—please, Shinobu. Stop," I said. "If you keep sucking, Hanekawa *will be gone* too. And I—don't want that."

And when I said those words.

Shinobu moved away from Hanekawa's neck with surprising nonchalance. Hanekawa's neck—had two clear fang marks carved into it, but I didn't need to worry about those. It was different from the bite mark on my own nape. Unlike with me, Shinobu only sucked the Afflicting Cat's vitality, in order to feed—she was simply eating.

Vampires suck human blood—but it means different things when they suck it for food and when they suck it to create thralls.

Maybe that was why Shinobu ran off.

So said the Afflicting Cat.

The aberration that had just been sucked away.

Shinobu plodded back toward me, done with her meal—and sank right back into my shadow.

Had she taken a liking to it?

Living in my shadow?

And then—

It was just me and a black-haired Hanekawa.

She wasn't conscious—her eyes shut, she was sleeping.

She probably wouldn't wake up until the next morning.

"………"

And with that, the incident was settled.

But—that of course didn't mean the problem was solved. We had rid her of the Afflicting Cat, but nothing else had changed—we had only eliminated the Afflicting Cat, and not her stress itself. Not only that, this new stress had taken shape over little more than a month—so there was no small chance it would reappear. Even if it didn't, Hanekawa had her longstanding family issues, so—

No.

That wasn't true.

Putting her family stuff aside.

What happened this time—was an issue I could do something about.

I could make things a little easier for Hanekawa starting from the very next day, all depending on how I behaved. Of course, I didn't think I could change the way I felt—but those feelings of wanting to repay her were certainly my own, too.

I wanted to save Hanekawa.

Her given name conjured up images of taking others under her wing, but that didn't mean I couldn't take her under mine.

I'd come and save her as I pleased.

No matter what anyone said, just as I pleased.

"Phew…"

A sigh left my lips.

I did have to admit, though, I was tired… My energy had been drained down close to its limit, after all. Even my mock-vampire body seemed like it was going to need time to recover. I doubted I'd be able to budge until the next morning, too. Sheesh, and I needed to be thanking everyone who'd helped out…

Well, it would be fine.

I did get to see Hanekawa in her pajamas.

In terms of "The North Wind and the Sun," this made me closer to the North Wind, but…there was no better sight than a black-haired, slow-breathing Hanekawa in her pajamas under a street lamp, as though a spotlight had been shone on her. Not only did her present state make me twice as happy, it felt like you could double my joy again on top of that. As compensation for the day's hard labor, it was bliss. Spending the night with Hanekawa there, as I watched her from the side of the road, didn't seem so bad now…

The stars in the sky.

They were so beautiful, after all.

"Mm, mmmh," Hanekawa made a sound.

Like she was talking in her sleep.

"Araragi…"

Or maybe—she wasn't talking in her sleep as much as words were spilling from her mouth in her hazy state of mind. Shinobu had sucked only the Afflicting Cat's existence from her, so perhaps she still had trouble separating Black Hanekawa and Hanekawa in her head, putting her in a state where the two intermingled.

So she wasn't talking in her sleep—she was giving voice to her feelings.

Tsubasa Hanekawa's unadorned, true feelings were spilling from her lips.

"What do you mean, paying me back is more important to you than our friendship—don't say that. What a sad, lonely thing to say."

"……"

Hanekawa kept her eyes closed—as she murmured the words.

"Araragi… You need to shape up."

And then—she fell back into a deep sleep.

My goodness, even when she slumbers.

Serious until the end—a master in the field.

It was no time to be worried about someone else.

Even so, my reply to her was immediate and candid, like a conditioned reflex. I hadn't been trained by Hanekawa in the two months since becoming a third-year for nothing. Despite it all, I knew how I needed to reply.

"Okay."

008

The epilogue, or maybe, the punch line of this story.

The next day, I was roused from bed as usual by my little sisters Karen and Tsukihi. *Hm?* I thought, tilting my head—which is when it came back to me. Right, I ended up not spending the night there on the side of the road. While that was dangerously close to happening ("dangerously" feels like the wrong word when I think about Hanekawa in her pajamas—maybe I should use a word that better celebrates my fortune instead), Suruga Kanbaru came storming in at an incredible speed using *takkyudo* or a flash step, while holding B to dash, or whatever it was she did, after a bit of time passed. After doing everything in my power to stop Kanbaru's throbbing heart—*so this is Hanekawa, that senior I've heard so much about*—I asked her to take Hanekawa back home. With how complicated her family situation is, it might be easier to come up with an excuse if a second-year girl took her home instead of me, a boy—saying it had something to do with the culture festival should be enough of a reason. No…even if that weren't the case, I didn't have the strength yet to walk her home. So I asked Kanbaru, *Could you call my two sisters? I'll give you their number.* I also asked her to look for Sengoku, but Kanbaru had met her a little earlier and had her go home because it was getting late. Another gal who didn't miss much. When I asked to make sure she hadn't seduced Sengoku, Kanbaru flashed me an embarrassed smile—hold on, that kind of smile wasn't the right answer.

And so, just as Kanbaru and Sengoku had done for me on Monday, my two little sisters supported me from both sides as we headed home, and then I slept—*you've been getting into too much trouble lately, Koyomi,* the older of the two reprimanded me. There was nothing I could say in my defense. Though at the same time, those two are the last people I'd want to hear that from…

Anyway, the next morning.

I headed toward the abandoned cram school before going to school—to deliver Shinobu, who'd been hiding in my shadow ever since, back to Oshino. I never did figure out why she absconded in the first place. I could ask her but she wouldn't reply, and she of course wasn't saying anything on her own. I could come up with a whole list of guesses, but it also felt like all of them were wrong. It could have even been that she wanted to make me sweat for troubling her too often lately—but that might be another wrong guess.

Oshino wasn't at the abandoned cram school.

He seemed to be out.

Come to think of it, I didn't know what Oshino's intentions were, either—why did he let the Afflicting Cat get away? Maybe she really did slip away when he wasn't looking, but he also could have turned a blind eye. Either way—it was the one time I found it impossible to believe he could have seen every single twist coming. He might have predicted that I'd act as a mousetrap by going out to find Shinobu and that she'd hide in my shadow, but why would he want the Afflicting Cat to bite me? Black Hanekawa had the intelligence of a cat, so what was the probability that she'd hit upon the truth of the situation?

However.

I had to say there was one thing he must have known—the root of Hanekawa's stress. He already knew by the time he asked his first question.

It wasn't that Oshino was special—it was just that I was so dense.

I was obtuse.

Less acute than anything I'd come across all day.

But if he wasn't around, he wasn't around.

If you can't help it, you can't help it.

And so I headed toward school, with Shinobu still hiding in my shadow. I did feel hesitant about bringing her there, but I hesitated even more to leave a vampire who now had a record of absconding alone by herself.

I met Hanekawa in class.

"Oh. You're later than usual," she said.

"Well, I took a detour on the way."

"Feeling well?"

"Feeling great."

"Good morning."

"Good morning.

That was it.

I still don't know how much of her memory she lost as Hanekawa, nor what she retains. I would have to ask her some time, but that time wasn't now. She needed some space to put her mind back in order.

As always, Senjogahara arrived at school moments before classes started as if she'd calculated it so as not to waste a single moment.

"Welcome home."

"Thanks."

"When's our next date?" she asked abruptly.

With the same flat and expressionless face as always.

"You plan it out, Araragi."

"......"

"I'll skin you alive if you take me anywhere lame."

"...Roger that."

In fact, I had a plan.

I'd show Senjogahara my treasure this time.

And crab, too—we had to go eat some eventually.

After classes, we prepared for the culture festival—the last one of my high school life. It was getting so close I could taste it, and today was the last day of preparations. Even Senjogahara didn't skip today and helped us strive toward our goal. It sounded like everyone stayed at school until some ridiculously late hour the day before, but now that Hanekawa, the class president, was back, the work proceeded at a completely different level of efficiency, and all of our classmates were free to go just before school officially closed for the day.

From there, I decided to give the abandoned cram school another visit and took along with me Senjogahara, Hanekawa, and also Kanbaru, who'd been waiting for us. I was the only one with a bike, so I pushed it and we all walked together.

Oshino wasn't there.

Yet again.

That's strange, Senjogahara said. *That man acts like he sees it all coming, and he isn't around for two of your visits in a row.* It made me realize that if anything was strange, it was that Senjogahara had come with me to meet Oshino, even if I had invited her. Maybe she'd already sensed this would happen. Maybe she'd figured it out by the time I explained it to her.

The four of us split up and searched every nook and cranny of the ruins, but Oshino was nowhere to be found. When we looked closely, very closely, however, it seemed that a few things were missing from inside the building—and they were all Oshino's belongings.

It was clear now.

Mèmè Oshino was gone.

Without leaving behind a single note—he'd left our town.

Now it made sense—when I'd biked to the cram school with Hanekawa the day before, it hadn't been to find Shinobu that he'd been outside. He'd been in the middle of packing up. He must have been undoing that spiritual boundary he'd set around the place.

On that occasion.

I hadn't been waited for.

The ruined shrine on top of the mountain—Oshino's interest in this town must have reached its endpoint when that case was settled. It was one of his biggest goals—that's how he described it.

His collecting and researching would some day come to an end—

He would leave this town some day—

And that turned out to be now.

I'm not going to disappear all of a sudden one day without even saying goodbye—I'm an adult—I do know my manners—

Why didn't I notice?

He was already saying goodbye with those words. How could you take them any other way? He was a man who never said goodbye, who couldn't deal with farewells, an awkward, tactless man, and it was the most earnest show of affection he could manage—

Honestly.

I really was dense.

I should have been able to figure that out.

There's no time, he'd told me.

So that was about Shinobu.

He looked the other way when Shinobu left, too—he knew, and he let her get away. He probably hadn't actively encouraged her, but he must have seen it as a fine opportunity. The Afflicting Cat joined the fray at a good moment—which is to say, a bad one—and so he just retroactively added her to the story. In other words, he saw Shinobu's disappearance as a test for me—or rather, as a sort of parting gift.

He became sure of something or another when I ran off to find Shinobu—and after he let the Afflicting Cat escape, he must have gathered his things and left. He was sure—that I'd manage to do something about both Shinobu and Hanekawa on my own.

That Hawaiian-shirted bastard.

Trying to act so suave.

He wasn't making me think he was cool.

A day had already passed, so Oshino must have already wandered into another town where he was busy with his collecting and researching—who knew, maybe he was saving someone from an attacking aberration as he happened to pass by.

Yes.

He was probably saving someone.

"Whatta…" I said.

"Yeah," Senjogahara said too.

"Totally," Hanekawa added.

"No mistake," Kanbaru agreed.

And then, all four of us in unison.

"Chump."

Mèmè Oshino—

A frivolous, cynical, vulgar, mean, arrogant, superficial, malicious, insincere, dramatic, jesting, capricious, selfish, lying, dishonest—and endlessly good and kind person.

And so, we each returned to our homes. Kanbaru left first, then Hanekawa split off, and then I walked Senjogahara home. There, for the first time, which is to say at last, Senjogahara treated me to her cooking. As far as my thoughts on the taste and her skills, well, let's say it was a smart move for her to leave it up to my imagination for so long.

I will probably encounter more aberrations in my life.

I can't pretend they never happened, and I can't forget them.

But—that's fine.

I know.

That there's darkness in the world, and that things live in the darkness.

For example, in my own shadow.

A blond kid, who seems very cozy there.

It was getting late by the time I got home, so I ate dinner, took a bath, and went straight to sleep. My two sisters would surely wake me up the next morning, just like they always do.

Tomorrow was finally the culture festival.

Our class was putting on: a haunted house.

Afterword

While there's no telling how many people have found themselves concerned about how to draw the line between their hobbies and their work, I believe the problem is such a difficult one because we start from the assumption that hobbies and work have the same absolute value. Hobbies. And work. I will admit, they are both major facets of one's life. When I think about it closely, though, it seems somehow unnatural that we treat the two as mutually exclusive. Or rather, some deep-rooted ethical notion that hobbies and work should never be one and the same seems to exist prior to the premise. It's said that you shouldn't make your hobby your work, but we can't survive without working. Meanwhile, life feels empty without hobbies. In that case, we in fact ought to encourage people to make their hobby their work, or their work their hobby, from an efficiency standpoint. So then why is it said that you shouldn't make your hobby your work? Probably thanks to a contradiction such as follows: seeing work, which we perform in order to live, in terms of enjoyment is inappropriate, while hobbies, which we have in order to live better, are meant to be enjoyed. But it's not as if making your hobby your work means that it stops being a hobby, and it's also not as if something ceases to count as work because you're doing it as a hobby. Your hobby is not your work, and your work is not your hobby. It is your hobby, and it is also your work. There may be nothing cooler than someone who can stand tall as a living example of this idea.

So, at the risk of being misunderstood, I'd like to say that *BAKEMONOGATARI* was written entirely as a hobby. There isn't a speck of anything work-related about it. It started as a novel I wrote as a diversion to fill a hole in my schedule, and I honestly wonder whether I should really be releasing it like this. Because I wrote it as nothing more than a hobby, I'm terribly ashamed that the author's favorite characters could be ranked far too easily, but I had so much fun penning scenes of any of the characters talking that, for the first time in a while, I was reminded of the days when I was just starting to write novels. As before, VOFAN was kind enough to adorn these pages with his work. I am of course reluctant to part ways with it, given that it was a hobby, but this brings an end to the five tales in these volumes. This has been *BAKE-MONOGATARI*, consisting of "Hitagi Crab," "Mayoi Snail," "Suruga Monkey," "Nadeko Snake," and "Tsubasa Cat."

Thank you very much for humoring my hobby.

NISIOISIN